Pushing the Limit

Also by Emmy Curtis

Dangerous Territory: An Alpha Ops Novella
Over the Line

Pushing the Limit

An Alpha Ops Novel

EMMY CURTIS

New York Boston

Copyright © 2014 by Emmy Curtis
Excerpt from *Over the Line* copyright © 2014 by Emmy Curtis
Cover design by Elizabeth Turner
Cover copyright © 2014 by Hachette Book Group, Inc.

Forever Yours
Hachette Book Group
1290 Avenue of the Americas
New York, NY 10104
hachettebookgroup.com
twitter.com/foreverromance

First published as an ebook and as a print on demand: November 2014

Forever Yours is an imprint of Grand Central Publishing.
The Forever Yours name and logo are trademarks of Hachette Book Group, Inc.

The publisher is not responsible for websites (or their content) that are not owned by the publisher.

The Hachette Speakers Bureau provides a wide range of authors for speaking events. To find out more, go to www.hachettespeakersbureau.com or call (866) 376-6591.

ISBN: 978-1-4555-3077-9 (ebook edition)
ISBN: 978-1-4555-3095-3 (print on demand edition)

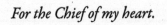

For the Chief of my heart.

Acknowledgments

I'd like to thank everyone who helped me get the details of EOD and JPAC missions correct; anything I've had to change to serve the story is entirely on me.

Thanks also to everyone on the Forever team: Leah Hultenschmidt, Julie Paulauski, Fareeda Bullert, Elizabeth Turner, Megha Parekh, and Jamie Snider. Their patience and humor is unending (hopefully).

To my husband, who inspired the whole Alpha Ops series, I give all my thanks and love for his constant support and patience.

A shout-out to my local writing stalwarts, Rachel Brune and Kristin Grimes: thanks for the writing dates and for making the drive on base...and for the coffee and cakes and stuff.

If you enjoy reading about Master Sergeant Matt Stanning and are interested in supporting the USAF community of EOD, please go here to see the good work the EOD Warrior Foundation does for the families of their fallen American heroes: eodwarriorfoundation.org.

The Joint POW/MIA Accounting Command's responsibility to bring back all fallen warriors from every war is detailed here, along with their current mission: www.jpac.pacom.mil.

"Until they are home."

—The Joint POW/MIA Accounting Command's Motto

Pushing the Limit

Chapter 1

The rehearsal dinner for the wedding from hell, three months ago

Thank you, God!

A tall, very handsome man approached her table at the back of the restaurant. This rehearsal dinner was out of control. Too many people, too much security, too few places to hide and drink. *Please let him be sitting here. Please let him be sitting here.* Harry looked at the place name next to hers: Matt Stanning.

She promised God she would go to church on Sunday if this delicious man sat next to her. There wasn't enough alcohol in the world to sit at a table with the bride's ex-boyfriend, his work colleagues, and as lovely as she was, Harry's ex-boyfriend's new fiancée and make it through the dinner without embarrassing herself.

She scratched at a hairpin sticking in her scalp. Why, oh why, couldn't she have pretended to be out of the country on a dig? Hell, she easily could have been really out of the country. But Sadie had been there for her all through college, been there afterward when Harry's world fell apart. She fingered Danny's wedding ring that she'd worn on a necklace since he died. He would be laughing at her, shoehorned into a glamorous dress at a fancy restaurant. So not like her.

"I'm Matt," the impossibly good-looking man said as he pulled out the chair next to Harry.

"Henrietta," she said, extending her hand.

He shook it but held on as he sat, sending an overt signal to her. God, he must be a player. She tried to extricate her hand, but he only released it when the waiter arrived to take his drink order. "Scotch for me, and whatever the ladies are having." He said, slipping the waiter a hundred-dollar bill. "And keep them coming."

Harry couldn't help but giggle. She leaned in and stage-whispered, "I think the drinks are free."

"But now we have our own drinks waiter," he whispered back.

Hallelujah. Harry threw both arms in the air. "Score!"

Beth, James's new fiancée, seemed to find her excitement amusing. But come on. It was a wedding, and she knew no one save the bride and the bride's brother—her ex, who also happened to be the son of the director of the CIA. "So what do you do, Matt?" Beth asked as Harry took a sip of her mojito.

He leaned back, shoved both hands behind his head, and smiled at the pair of them. "I can turn my hand to most things."

Beth snorted into her drink. "Unbelievable."

He tipped his head to the side. "What? You don't believe me? I swear I'm pretty handy to have around."

So cocky. Now Harry wanted to take him down. She touched his arm in what she hoped he would take as a come-on. "Oh, honey. I can see you are. You obviously think you're very capable. But some women don't need men for anything."

Instead of deflating him, her pushback seemed to interest

him. He sat forward, arms resting on his legs. "Nothing at all? I find that hard to believe."

Harry pretended to think, finger on her chin as she appeared to consider the one thing she could possibly need from a man. "Well, maybe I can think of one thing. One...very delicate task that I frequently need help with..."

His eyes traced her face and trended down to her legs. Beth was right. Unbelievable. If his dark eyes weren't so mesmerizing she would have left him to deal with Beth. But despite his incredible overconfidence, something compelled her to stay. There was something in his eyes. Like maybe he was playing a role. *Yeah, like maybe that's just wishful thinking.*

She dropped her voice as if imparting a huge secret. "Often, in the middle of the night"—she looked around the table furtively—"I get this feeling"—she pressed her hand to her stomach and rubbed it slowly—"and I wish I had someone with me to"—an Oscar-winning pause—"open the pickle jar."

Matt laughed out loud, throwing his head back. "I'll admit, you had me in the palm of your hand there." He shook his head at her. "Man, I definitely owe you a drink for that."

"So what brings you to the wedding of the year?" Harry asked.

"I'm a friend of the groom. I was supposed to be out of town, but my plans were canceled, so here I am. You?" He pulled in his chair a bit and put his napkin in his lap.

She pulled a sad face. "Maid of honor. Bride's friend from college. I should have been away, too." Well, she'd *wanted* to be away, at least. "So here we both are."

"Indeed." He took the scotch that the waiter had left and gulped almost half of it down. Peering at the glass, he said, "This is the good stuff. Very smooth."

"I don't think Sadie's parents actually know there are things in this world that aren't the good stuff. This whole shindig should be one for the record books."

"Well, I've never actually been to a wedding before, so I wouldn't know," he said.

"Really? I thought I was the only one who'd managed to be away for everyone's weddings. This is exactly my second one ever."

"And how does this compare?" he asked.

"Well, the first was mine, and I got married on a beach...so this one is in a league of its own as far as I'm concerned."

"You're married?" She saw him peek at her ringless hand. At least he bothered to check. A lot of guys don't really care.

"Not anymore." She thought it best to keep the murky details to herself. No point in bringing the party down with her sad story. "You?"

"Nope." He laughed. "Never even come close. I move too fast." His player grin came back. She wanted to slap it off his face. She was more and more convinced that he was smoke-screening. She knew because she was an expert at it.

"How so?"

He looked surprised to be called out on it. "I just travel too much to put down roots."

Harry wanted to know what he did, but she had this feeling that by getting him to spill all his details, she would somehow be compelled to do the same. Life was too short.

"So are you here for the whole weekend?" Suddenly she had to shout to be heard over the chatter in the room that had almost reached critical mass. She looked around. There seemed to be more people in here than the tables could possibly fit. She was jostled by someone walking behind their chairs.

Matt turned all his attention to Harry. "I'm going to slip out for a smoke. Want to come?"

"You smoke?"

"Nope." He stood and made to pull out Harry's chair, too. What? She looked up at him, puzzled. And then she felt a kick on her ankle. Beth gave her a meaningful look and nodded her head toward the door with a grin.

"Okay, sure?"

He helped her up with a hand under her elbow and steered her through the throng of people to the restaurant's patio. He opened the French door and held it for her to go through.

As soon as the door closed behind him, he took a deep breath.

"Are you all right?" she asked, still puzzled by his actions.

"I'm fine." He took another deep breath and looked out over the gardens. "Wow. Who would have expected this oasis in the middle of D.C.?"

* * *

As soon as her attention was diverted by the picturesque garden, he took several silent, deep, slow breaths. *Come on, Matt. Hold it together.* He tried to concentrate on Henrietta. She was stunning. Petite, blond, with a vibrancy that seemed to pulse out of her. She was exactly his type. Exactly the distraction he needed.

Usually he was able to pick up a woman before the crowds came. Bar, nightclub, party…get there early and close the deal before he got too claustrophobic. It was just the noise and the thrum behind the chatter. Made him edgy. It was like every wave of sound and energy chipped away at his sanity. It was normal, given what he'd been through. Nothing to worry about.

The garden was lit up with low-level solar lights casting

shadows in the night. The air was cooler than when he had arrived, suggesting the forecast storm was indeed going to pass through the area. But here he was. Away from the tightness he'd felt at the table.

"You're right. It's beautiful out here. I hear the chef grows his own herbs and vegetables in these gardens," she said, walking along one of the many paths that snaked out into the garden from the patio.

He followed her while he could still see her in the dim light. The fragments of laughter and music from the restaurant diminished with each step. Damp air and darkness swallowed him up the farther they went into the garden. He lost sight of her in a mini-orchard of mature fruit trees.

Suddenly her voice came from his left. "If you don't smoke, what made you want to come out here?"

Out of the corner of his eye he saw her sitting on what looked like a stone bench under a tree. SERE school had taught him that peripheral vision was stronger in the darkness. It had saved him more than once during the Survive, Evade, Resist, and Escape training he'd undertaken years earlier.

"You must have great night vision," he countered, trying to change the subject. He picked his way through the plants to get to her.

"I have to in my line of work," she answered softly, as if a loud voice would shatter the peace.

"What do you do that requires good night vision?" he asked as he sat in the middle of the bench. No use being polite and sitting as far away from her as he could.

"I'm an archaeologist. All tunnels, crypts, and cold dark tents in the middle of fields."

"That must be interesting. And dirty, and cold."

"All of those." She laughed.

He was well aware of how archaeologists work. He worked with a lot of them. "What made you want to be one?" he asked.

She hesitated, and for the first time he sensed he had somehow touched a nerve.

"I was left some money when I was young, so I decided to use it to study. I decided…" She stopped again.

He didn't fill in the silence. He never did.

"Initially, I just liked the past. I decided that I could live in the past quite easily if I elected to study it. And soon it became the love of the job. The discoveries, the frustrations, the investigating. It's like a drug to me."

"I get that. Completely." She had just described his feelings about his job precisely. He protected teams who did what she did. He investigated, dug, and enjoyed moments of elation followed by intense sorrow at what they'd found.

"So why did you want to come out for a smoke?" Her voice firm in the darkness. She clearly wasn't going to let that one go.

"I like being outside. Away from people," he said, taking a subconscious move away from her on the bench. *Fuck. Where had that come from?* "Well, at least these people. Too rich for me," he recovered.

"I'm not one of those too-rich people?" she asked softly.

He smiled in the dark. "I know you're not. You've been scratching the pins in your hair since I first saw you. And as you walked the path, you kept smoothing the sides of your dress, like it was unfamiliar. I'd say you're dressed for the occasion, not the lifestyle." He leaned his elbows on his knees and looked at her in the dark. "Am I wrong?"

She paused. "No, not wrong at all. This is the first time I've worn a bra and a dress in about three years."

What? Did he hear that right? He half laughed, half coughed. "What?"

"You heard. I'm usually in shorts and a tank top. And these girls do not merit a bra, as I'm sure you've already noticed." She sounded rueful.

When he'd first seen her he'd thought she was ideal for him, almost feline in her petite frame. Women have a very skewed impression of what men like. Or maybe it was just him. "You looked flawless to me. I just wish I could see you better in the dark."

"That's easy. Let's see if your fingers are as observant as your eyes." She took his hands in hers and stood to rearrange herself. "Come on."

Speechless, he stood with her and sat when she did, astride the stone bench so their knees touched.

"My best friend at high school was blind. She taught me to see with my hands," she said, placing his fingers on her forehead. "Close your eyes and touch me."

His brain just about exploded. How did he go from wanting to take Henrietta home to here, having her ask him to touch her? He hesitated, struggling with the thought that this might be an elaborate hallucination. How else did you go from chatting at a wedding to feeling up a beautiful woman in the dark? *Hell. Just go with it.*

Her hands rested on his knees as she tipped her face up slightly. His fingertips traced her forehead and hairline, ears, eyelashes. Her skin felt like warm silk. "You're beautiful," he said, cursing his gravelly tone. He was as hard as fuck, and he didn't know why. He wasn't some damn teenager. Strangely, touching her felt completely right and slightly wrong at the same time.

"May I?" she asked in the dark, and raised her hands to his

face before he agreed. Her touch was warm against his skin. He closed his eyes again and just concentrated on her fingers.

"You feel tense to me. As if you spend too much time frowning. Do you have a stressful job?"

He used to, that was for sure. He used to be an EOD airman. The one they bring in when they find explosives. The one who has to detonate bombs safely in a war zone. The one who has a two in three chance of not making it home. He'd been young and figured he was invincible. They all had. Until they weren't. Until he'd lost his best friend because they'd been messing around.

After another couple of years of EOD, he'd been sent to JPAC, the Joint POW/MIA Accounting Command. The dry name for a team of people who scaled mountains, hiked deserts, and parachuted into inhospitable areas to find missing troops. Didn't matter how long they'd been missing, one year or eighty years. They went to get them. It was his atonement for leaving Danny in Iraq. Well, most of him.

His heart clenched at the wound inside that just would not heal. It had been seven years, and he still lived with his loss every day. Was it supposed to be like this?

"What's wrong?" Henrietta's hands stilled over his tight lips and then dropped to his hands. She wove her fingers between his rigid ones. "Tell me about it."

Hell, no. Hell. No. "I'd rather talk about you." That was a lie. All he wanted to do was lose himself. To forget. Before he could second-guess his motivation, he leaned forward and snaked his hand into her hair and pulled her toward him.

She hesitated for the smallest second before he felt her hair tumbling down over his hand. She must have been really ready to lose those pins. Her cool heavy hair caressed his hand and arm, and the scent of vanilla invaded the space between them.

He could think of nothing else but tasting her lips. He opened his legs wider and roughly brought her closer. She took a shaky breath when he was a mere inch from her mouth. As she exhaled he pulled her head to his. His tongue swiped at her lower lip before he pressed his mouth to hers. Her tongue touched his lips, and he nearly exploded. He stroked her tongue with his as he held her head at the perfect angle between his two hands.

Her fingers gripped his knees as if she was scared to fall. Then they inched up his thigh. Jesus. He was so hot for her. The air turned oppressively heavy as their breathing became more labored. She found his erection through his pants and pressed against it.

He groaned against her mouth. Somewhere in his head the words "Game On" flashed like a neon bar sign. He dragged his hands down her back to her zipper and pulled it to her ass. His hands slipped inside the dress and felt the skin on her back.

She moaned and arched her back pulling her mouth from his. He slipped the dress down from her shoulders so it pooled at her waist. As if God had intended, the moon peeked out from the clouds and illuminated her perfectly. His heart nearly stopped. She was beautiful. Her lacy bra barely covered her pert breasts, and she gave off an incredibly hot wanton air, sitting in front of him half-naked. Her eyes fluttered open, and she held his gaze, unembarrassed.

His hands moved by their own volition to cover her from prying eyes, but there weren't any; they were completely secluded. Her light eyes took him to a different place—one free of distractions or anxiety.

Thunder rumbled overhead, but neither looked away. She reached up and loosened his tie enough that she could slip it over his head. Then she unbuttoned his shirt. He let her. He knew he shouldn't. He knew someone could come out at any moment. And then a drop of rain fell on her, sliding down her collarbone over the swell of her breast and into her bra. Followed by another and another.

Maybe no one would be coming out at all.

Neither of them moved, she didn't even flinch as the rain came down steadier. "Take off your shirt," she said. "I want to see you."

His hands went automatically to the sides of his shirt. He hesitated. "Take off your bra. I want to see *you*."

Henrietta took it off in one move. Hell, he'd never met a woman like her before. Fearless. He shucked off his shirt and they looked at each other for a moment. Rain fell steadily. The cool water made her nipples erect. He wanted to get his mouth on them so bad his mouth watered.

She drew patterns on his chest with her fingernails, playing with the raindrops on him.

He grabbed her hips and yanked her onto his lap. Her legs wrapped around his waist as her lips descended on his. He never wanted to leave this spot. It felt like a dream. Almost an out-of-body sensation, with the rain, the lightning in the distance, and the incredible half-naked woman in front of him. *She must be a dream.*

His lips tracked kisses down her neck to her breasts and as the tip of his tongue touched her already hard nipple, she gasped and arched into him. His dick stiffened even more, pressing against the heat behind her panties. His control was attached to him by the finest thread as he sucked on her, delighting in the gasps and moans threading their way around the garden.

It would take the merest hesitation to be balls-deep in her. Just the unzipping of his fly, the rip of a foil packet, and he could be sliding inside her velvet. As he gently twisted the nipple his mouth wasn't around, she ground her pussy against his pants.

Fuck, what was stopping him? This wasn't right. Maybe his brain wanted to lay her on silk sheets, take her to dinner, discover more about this incredible woman. Maybe that was it?

Really? He wanted to save her for the best, like a damn suit for church? Hell to that. He wanted to hear the noise she made when she came for him. He inched his way back from her a little, just enough that he could slide a hand between them. She bucked when he touched her panties, her heels digging into his butt. He traced the edges of the thin scrap of material that lay between him and heaven. She tensed and went completely still. As his fingers passed under the silk, she sighed and melted around him. His fingers gently stroked her folds, she seemed completely bare down there, and that excited him more than he would have ever imagined. He wanted to see her so bad. Naked.

As if in time with nature, thunder crashed as he stroked her from clit to ass, reveling in the heavy wetness that his fingers slipped through. He pressed at her ass gently, then slid back. He shifted to one side and eased two fingers into her. She moaned and found his mouth with hers. As he pulsed his fingers inside her, his thumb found her clit, pressed and used the wetness there to slip over it again and again until she tensed, gripped his fingers, and spasmed as her soft throaty sounds enveloped them both.

"Amazing," Henrietta whispered. "You made me feel amazing. My skin is vibrating."

"To be fair, that could be the rain." He laughed as she stretched her arms over her head and lengthened her spine like a cat. He could watch her forever. His.

No!

Not his. Hell, he didn't even know whose she was. She got up and pulled one leg around and sat next to him, back straight like a schoolteacher oblivious to the fact that she was still naked. "And now I want to make you vibrate for me," she breathed as she reached for his fly.

He wanted to stop her, wanted to be the better man here, but he was consumed by the moment. Rational thought was definitely still alive and well in his head, but so was his utter need to ignore it.

She unzipped him and took his dick in her rain-wet hand. Her firm grip almost undid him right there. Normally he wouldn't care so much how long he lasted. The women who got in his pants rarely saw him again. It was always just sex at its very basest level—a release. An escape. Nothing more.

He ground his teeth together to hold on to his control. But having her in his sight was almost his undoing. Still stripped from the waist up, she leaned over him, touching his dick to her breasts, teasing her own nipples with it. He swallowed hard.

He closed his eyes and instantly felt the sharp touch of her teeth and the softness of her tongue on him. She swirled her tongue over its tip and then slid down so he was totally in her mouth. He groaned with a primal need for her. A need he doubted would be sated anytime now.

As she pulled up, she sucked slowly and squeezed his balls. A stream of fire filled his entire body. She sucked down his shaft again, pausing and then sliding him in right to the back of her throat. Every instinct made him want to hold her head and fuck her mouth. Control. He had control.

A door slammed, and a spark of a lighter came from the restaurant patio. She paused in response. Two men started a conversation under the awning. Sitting up and looking in the direction of the restaurant, she put her hand on his dick, stroking gently.

And then Henrietta started twisting her hand around his shaft, and his whole body sat in suspense. His muscles tightened. They were so close to being discovered. It made him hot as hell. Then she stood up properly, and her dress dropped to the ground, leaving her bare to him. She paused a moment, giving him the chance to burn her incredible image into his memory forever. Henrietta, in a thong, high heels, and nothing else.

She pushed him back so he was lying along the length of the stone seat. She bent over him and took him straight in her mouth again. With one hand, she held the base of his cock steady, with the other she caressed his balls. As she sucked up and down his length her small breasts bobbed in front of his eyes. Stars peeked out from the clouds, the rain stopped suddenly. It was like heaven was showing itself to him. He croaked, "I'm going to come."

She gently increased the pressure on his balls and took him in the tight vacuum of her mouth. She sucked up his length once, twice, and then he exploded as fireworks popped in his head. A tiny rational thought wondered if he was having an aneurysm, but he was in so much ecstasy that he embraced it.

He wanted nothing but to hold her in his arms, feel her naked body along the length of his, touch her all over. She'd been almost nude, but he still felt deprived of something much better. He sighed as she kissed her way up his stomach. Henrietta had turned him into a chick.

"Harry! Are you out here?" A woman's voice came from the patio.

"I'll be right there!" She yelled back in a surprisingly loud voice for such a tiny thing.

He leaned up on his elbows and watched her zip her dress back up. Man. He saw the faintest smudge of ink on her back. He wished it wasn't so dark.

"Harry?" he asked.

"My friends call me Harry."

"What can I call you?"

She grinned over her shoulder as she retreated down the path. "Henrietta."

Chapter 2

Iraq, present day

Harry lightly fingered the artifact in her pocket as she watched her grad students at work. Okay, she was pretty sure it wasn't an important artifact, historically anyway. But it was still an unusual find.

About three inches square, it was a piece of metal with embossed numbers. When she'd taken a photo and sent it to her lab, they had discovered the numbers were a code for an aircraft part. A military aircraft part.

She wondered if the piece had fallen from the sky, or if there was a plane crash, or if it was just incidental detritus. As an archaeologist, she was very aware that the discovery of one artifact didn't necessarily mean the rest of it was close by. Someone could have dropped it. Or sold it to someone who dropped it.

But to be safe, she'd e-mailed her friend at the Department of Defense, Sadie, and passed on word of her discovery. It was out of her hands now. But she couldn't help but touch the piece of metal. It had become a touchstone. A talisman of sorts.

She held down a button on her walkie-talkie. "That's the furthest north side of our site, so mark that please." Molly and Jason pulled small red flags from a backpack and placed them at intervals along the line of sight.

Harry checked the laptop and stopped them. "That's the western border, there." She did the same when they reached the other two sides of their site and then called them back. They hopped on their little ATV, and Harry smiled when she saw Molly wrap her arms firmly around Jason's waist. Molly had driven the ATV a hundred times before and definitely did not need to hold on to anyone. Maybe recruiting Jason was more than just a good thing for Harry's business.

She handed them bottles of water from the cooler when they got back to their small trailer-turned-lab pop-up to the south of their site. Then she threw one at Mueen, who sat on top of the trailer. He was their armed security guard. Quiet, unassuming, with a slight American accent borne of studying at UPenn, he was ever vigilant for problems, looters, or anyone that he deemed a threat to the team.

Harry had worked with him before on her first visit to Iraq. He and his wife had been pillars of strength for her, coming for the first time to the country where her husband had died. And thanks to them, she'd felt almost at home there. She'd been delighted and excited when she'd heard she'd been chosen for this job, mostly so that she could see her friends again.

"The site doesn't seem very big," Jason said.

Harry smiled at the newbie. "It's plenty big for the three of us, trust me."

"But we're not excavating or anything, are we?" he asked,

sitting on the blue-and-white cooler and taking a hefty slug of water.

Harry pulled up an image on the laptop and swiveled the screen so it faced them. "We will be working the site in a grid. In each square, we will take samples, survey for anomalies, and do a cursory check for surface artifacts. In places I've marked, here and here, we will auger boreholes to test the composition of the earth. At the end of the two weeks, we will use geo-phys across the whole site. That's all we're here for this time. If we find something interesting, chances are we'll be invited back to investigate further before the team of university archaeologists take over. And if we don't. Then we still will have earned our money."

Her Blackberry pinged and she elected to check her e-mails in the cool of the trailer. Harry left the students chatting outside about how to attack the grid in the most efficient way and escaped inside. She was actually itching to get back to their hotel this evening. She hadn't slept well since she found the piece of aircraft part right where they had set up the trailer. Above all things, she wanted a long sleep.

The inbound e-mail was from Sadie telling her that the Pentagon was sending someone to look at the site. An advance man from the JPAC team in Hawaii. Sadie explained that the people at JPAC were in charge of finding the remains of U.S. military service members and bringing them back to their families.

Harry closed the e-mail and shivered. This was the last thing she needed. But as someone who had lost a husband to war, she couldn't begrudge him access to the site. She hoped the artifact was just an anomaly. That a downed aircraft wasn't hiding in the dunes somewhere. Immediately her body flushed with shame. But her priority was to her client, a foundation that funded important archaeological digs for universities around the world. The U.S. government definitely didn't have any authority over her work here, and she didn't want to be put in a position where she'd have to choose between her work and a grieving family.

She knew how slowly the military worked, so she hoped the advance man wouldn't be here until they had finished. She closed her e-mail when her eyes started blurring. Sleep. She really needed sleep. Time to wrap today up.

There was a knock at the door. Mueen. Jason and Molly would have just burst in. She grabbed her backpack and the padlock for the door and opened it. Indeed, it was Mueen, and as always, he'd anticipated her every need.

"Are you ready to leave, madam?" he asked.

"We are." She turned to the others. "Let's load the truck and go back to the hotel. I, for one, need an early night."

They visibly brightened, and she wondered if they were planning on spending their personal time together. Her mind skipped back three months to Sadie's wedding. And Matt. The man she'd very nearly had sex with in a city restaurant's garden. He'd been outstanding. Really outstanding. Handsome, charming, a real player, too, yet strangely he hadn't tried to have sex with her. But that night still lived on in her daydreams. She sighed. Maybe she'd dream about him tonight. Kill two birds with one stone: the need for sleep and the need for sex.

But by the time they'd gotten back, eaten, and gone to their rooms, sleep was evasive yet again. If she believed in curses, she would have thought the metal on her bedside table was hexing her sleep abilities. The only other time sleep had evaded her for weeks was just after Danny had died. For weeks, every time she closed her eyes, all she saw was his smiling face and then an explosion as he evaporated into thin air. *The pretty pink mist as he evaporated.*

Gah. She sat up in the dark and pulled on a long-sleeved t-shirt and jeans and quickly braided her hair. Maybe a brandy in the hotel bar would help.

* * *

Air Force Senior Master Sergeant Matt Stanning stretched as he got off the army transport he'd hitched a ride on. As the humidity of the night settled heavily on his body, and the familiar smell of Iraq's dusty air assaulted his memory he tensed. He hadn't been back since his last tour as part of an Explosive Ordinance Disposal team. His tour in the Iraq theater had ended the week after they'd gathered the pieces of his best friend Danny McCantry and transported the parts of him they could find back to the U.S.

He'd been on his way back from a conference when they'd asked him to stop by here and check out something an archaeologist had found that suggested that there may have been a downed military aircraft in the vicinity. He doubted it strongly, since none of the records he'd looked at on the plane reported any unrecovered American plane crashes. Fucking checking the box. That's all he was here for. And he couldn't think of a worse place to come for a pointless exercise. He heaved his pack onto his back and tried to ignore the crush of people in the arrivals area, the constant clamor of noise that sent unease creeping up his spine like a desert viper.

"Boomer! Boomer!" A voice penetrated the fog that was settling around his brain. He was slow to react to the old call sign, but not slow to react to the hand on his arm. In a second he dropped his bag, grabbed the hand with his, and spun out so the person attached to the hand was now facing away from him with his arm twisted halfway up his back.

"Damn it, Boomer. Let me go," the man hissed, trying to look behind him.

In a flash Matt recognized David Church and let him go. "Sweet hell, Nitro. You don't grab someone like that."

David rubbed his shoulder. "Yeah, sorry. I've been out of uniform too long, apparently."

"Jesus." Matt dragged his hand over his face, unwilling to admit his fight instinct was still front and center. "What are you doing here?" Matt asked, grabbing his pack and then steering them through the throng of passengers and greeters who were now very definitely interested in the two men.

When they reached the relative calm of the taxi stand, Church filled him in. "I went private, man. I'm in MGL Security. We're contracted to look after you guys in country."

"Well, it's good to see you brother, but I don't need a security detail. I'm my own security detail."

"You don't say," Nitro said, rubbing his shoulder again. "I'm going to fuck you up if you damaged a nerve."

There was a pause, and then the two men laughed and briefly hugged, thumping fists on each other's back. "It's good to see you, too," Church said. "It's been too long. What was it? 2005?" He shook his head. "That was some fucked-up shit. Danny, man. What the fuck." He sighed.

This was absolutely, 100 percent not the conversation he wanted to have here and now. "Hey. Everything was fucked up. It was a long time ago. Things change."

Church pointed to a black Suburban. "This is my ride. It's bulletproof," he reassured as he got in the driver's seat.

Shit on a stick. Talk about standing out like a frigging sore thumb. He'd planned on getting an average, beat-up, barely running cab to the hotel. And this? This was not subtle.

"Too fucking right it's bulletproof. You're like a moving target. Nothing says 'invading American' quite like a big American car. Jesus, Nitro. What happened to you?"

Church put on a pair of aviators, pulled a toothpick from behind his ear, and stuck it in his mouth, all the while grinning at Matt's discomfort. "I'll tell you what happened. I sold out for the big bucks. You'll never get rich riding it out as an enlisted troop."

Matt watched the street scene as they left the airport complex. As soon as they got outside, arid desert stretched as far as he could see. His fists clenched. It was along roads like these that insurgents set their bombs in cars, old deflated soccer balls, children's toys... or just barely buried by the blowing sand. It was the ball that had got Danny.

"I have some gear for you in the back." Church said.

Matt turned in his seat and looked at the duffel bag. "Any booze?"

"Two Glocks, fifteen clips, a rifle and mags, a Canadian ID, just in case you get taken, a bottle of Jack Daniel's best, and a satellite phone. Hold down the pound key to get a direct line to me."

"You're not going to babysit me?"

"Nah. I was told to hold back, come when needed. I guess they figured you could take care of yourself."

"God bless you, Nitro."

"For the phone?"

"For the JD."

Church grinned back at him and offered a fist to bump. Matt hesitated and then complied. They both laughed again. Man, he wished his whole team could be back together, but they'd never had so much as a reunion after Danny had died. Would have been weird.

"I already checked you into your room at the hotel, and we swept the room. Everything looked fine."

"Thanks, but my mission here isn't covert, or even important. Just liaising on a rumor. You know I'm with JPAC now, right?"

"They briefed me. When did you leave EOD?"

"A few years back. You know how it goes. A man my age can't live on adrenaline alone."

"I definitely get that, brother. So what do you live on now?" he asked as he pulled into the hotel's dusty driveway.

"Women. JD. A satisfying job." It sounded weak even to him. But as he thought briefly about women, Henrietta came to mind, in the rain, sitting on top of him and leaning back to feel the rain on her body. Wait, she was an archaeologist. Maybe he could use that as an excuse to call her. Get her number from Simon and Sadie, say he needed her professional advice.

Food for thought.

Church handed him his room key. "Number thirteen. Figured fewer people would have been in it."

Matt took the key with a low laugh. No one was more superstitious than an EOD technician. He stood in the doorway of the Suburban and hesitated before he closed it. "Let's get together for a drink before I head off again."

"Hit the pound key, baby!" Nitro said as he revved the engine.

He slammed the door and watched him roar off, sunglasses still on despite the onset of dusk.

A gust of wind followed in his wake. Strong enough to make Matt wince and turn away from the splatter of sand against his face. When it abated, he looked at the sky and saw the telltale fast-moving clouds across the moon.

A storm was brewing.

Chapter 3

Harry sat in the corner of the bar sipping a glass of red wine, face to the wall. The hotel really only catered to foreign workers, and she had no wish to attract anyone's attention. She flipped over her black Megellin Foundation folder and reexamined the briefing on the project requirements for her and her team. Now they'd staked their area, she rethought the plan she'd given Jason and Molly. Their first whole day there tomorrow would now be geo-phys, instead of leaving it until last. She hoped that the results from the ground-penetrating radar that scanned three feet under the surface would head the military off at the pass and they could get on with their work.

She turned her attention back to the briefing pack. It was a slightly unusual remit. They weren't asking her to age any artifacts, just to scan the area and report back. It was a little strange, but their money was good, so less work for more money...well, it didn't happen often. Only once before, if memory served.

Recrossing her legs under the table, she drained the last of the wine. It was nearly midnight. God only knew why she couldn't sleep. She was too used to traveling to be bothered by jetlag. She was so sleepy, yet unable to sleep.

"Can I buy you a cocktail...Henrietta?"

She jumped and turned around. She blinked in disbelief. "Matt?"

"You are a sight for sore eyes, darlin', and I mean that literally." He slid in the booth next to her, making her shift around to face him. His eyes looked like they'd been sandblasted, they were so red.

"What are you doing here?" Briefly she wondered if she was hallucinating, or dreaming. But no. He leaned in and kissed her cheek and she could smell his skin, all soapy musk. Definitely not an apparition. Her heart rate made a definite uptick.

"I could say the same of you. I was literally thinking about you as I arrived here, and an hour later, here you are. It's like I picked up a genie on my travels."

"I don't understand..." Harry shook her head, almost in a daze.

He took a swallow of his beer. "I want to make a comment about all the gin joints in all the world, but I guess I stumbled into yours, not the other way around."

Harry bit back a smile. "You know you didn't have to come here. If you'd wanted to take me out for a drink you could have just asked."

"But this is so much more fun than just asking Simon for your number, isn't it." Crazy. Surely this was too much of a coincidence.

"Seriously, what do you do that would bring you here?" she asked, still wondering about being asleep and dreaming, or maybe even hallucinating due to lack of sleep.

He looked serious for a second. "I can't really tell you." He looked at her as if he were trying to gauge her reaction to his nonresponse.

"Do you work for the government?" She frowned, trying to make sense of the whole situation. "Wait. You must do something like that. Didn't you help with the attack at Sadie and Simon's aborted wedding? I was stuck in the bathroom most of the time, but I think I heard...that *was* you, wasn't it?" Sadie and Simon's wedding, the day after the rehearsal dinner where they'd met, didn't exactly go off smoothly. It didn't happen at all. Armed gunmen stormed the house and kind of put an end to any thoughts of a romantic wedding. Not to mention the bride's brother being shot.

"Funny." He nodded slowly, taking a deliberate pause. "I was there, all right. Just in time to see you running off with the brother of the bride."

Urgh. She cringed. "Yes. That wasn't my finest moment. It really wasn't what it looked like."

"So you weren't completely devastated at the thought that you might lose him?"

She paused. "I wasn't devastated. James being shot...shocked me. But I realize now that it was just that: shock. I thought it was something else, but it wasn't." Hell. She looked at her glass. In vino veritas. She wanted to admit that she hadn't really felt anything after the initial shock dissipated. But, she didn't want him to think of her as that...cold. She changed the subject. "So *are* you with the government?"

"I am. Do you trust me now?" He gave that player smile that had so intrigued her at the rehearsal dinner.

She relaxed into the corner between the vinyl cushion of her booth seat and the wall. "Not even slightly," she said. "And you can get me another red wine, if you're up." She looked at him, still seated.

A split second later he figured out what she meant, and he jumped up. "I'm up. I'm up."

Harry felt a frisson of pleasure rush through her as she watched him at the bar. Of all the gin joints, indeed. Maybe this would mean they could actually seal the deal this time. And she was only in Iraq for two weeks, so she wouldn't have to declare everlasting love or anything unsavory like that. No awkward conversations explaining that she'd already met, and lost, the love of her life, that she wasn't looking for love or commitment, white picket fences, or happy families. For a second she remembered the feel of his hands and eyes on her, being practically naked for him in the garden, in the rain.

He returned with her wine and this time sat opposite her. He jumped straight in. "You told me you're an archaeologist, right? What are you excavating here?"

"Nothing. We're just doing some forward prep work for a foundation that finances student archaeological digs. Obviously the students have a finite time in which they can work and get credits outside the classroom, so occasionally my company takes the job of surveying and prepping a site for them." Slowly, she swirled her wine about the glass, thinking about the shard of metal that they'd found just setting up the trailer on the site.

He cleared his throat. "Have you found anything interesting? Anything to report?" The question was breezy, casual even, but she immediately knew who he was and why he was there.

Aha. "What kind of thing do you mean?" she asked, probing.

He leaned back in his chair and smiled.

"You're my liaison?"

* * *

Bingo. And boy was he up for a bit of liaising. "I guess I am. You haven't told anyone about your discovery, have you?" Instinctively his eyes flickered from one barfly to the next, checking their level of interest in either Henrietta or him.

"God, no. My assistants and our security guard know, but they know better than to tell anyone. Anything we find, be it ancient or modern, is kept secret until it can be secured from looters or other…interested people. It's an absolutely normal protocol in my line of work." She frowned.

"That's good. That's the same SOP as we have. No one talks about anything until we can secure it." He drank some beer.

"I thought maybe I'd have a couple of weeks before someone came," she said.

"Normally it would take that long, maybe longer. Usually there is a whole process to go through before we set boots on the ground. But I have an Iraqi visa, and I was in Kuala Lumpur at a conference, so they just diverted me here on the way back."

"You've been to Iraq before?" Her fingers slid around the glass, barely touching it, and he felt it as if she were tracing those designs on his skin. His dick twitched in his pants. *Really?* Shit, he hadn't slept for thirty hours and he was still interested?

"Of course. We had a war here not so long ago. You?"

"Once before. I was part of a dig close to Ur, southeast of here."

"I know Ur. The ziggurat, right?" He remembered the huge stepped pyramid-like building outside the town of Nasiriyah.

She grinned. "Wow, a soldier who knows the ziggurat. Beautiful isn't it?"

"I'm an airman," he said, "And yes, it was. Agatha Christie

wrote some of her books there, right? While her husband excavated?" He swore her face fell a little when he said he was an
airman. Strange. Most women heard that and thought "fighter
pilot." He'd gotten a lot of ass because of *Top Gun*.

"Yes, she did," she replied absently.

He steadied her hand that was now tapping on the table by
placing his on top of it. "Are you okay?" Her skin was velvet under
his fingers. He wanted to relive that night in the garden, her wet
body driving him crazy. He thanked God he'd been given this
second chance to possess her, to close the deal once and for all.
The opportunity to get her out of his system, because hell, had
she been in his system since he'd met her.

"I'm fine. Just tired." She looked up and smiled. "I am happy
to see you, though. How long are you planning on staying?"

"Depends. Maybe just tonight. I need to send details of the"—
he looked around—"apple, back to HQ."

"Apple?"

"First thing that came to mind. Maybe something to do with
how tempting you look to me." Did he just say that? Well, she
was tempting, all looking like she just got out of bed, messily
braided blond hair and sweatshirt with a neck just baggy enough
to allow him sight of a pristine-white bra strap. *So she did wear
a bra sometimes.* She looked innocent, and he knew she was anything but. Still, he wanted to corrupt her in the worst way. Her
angelic looks just made him want her more.

Her eyelids lowered a fraction as she held his gaze. He loved
that she didn't demure, or deny, his attraction. Try to negate the
compliment the way women sometimes did.

"Do you want to... come up and see my apple?" she asked with
a barely perceptible wink. Her mouth twitched as if she was hiding a smile.

"Yes. Yes, I really would."

"I'm in room twenty-three. Give me a few minutes, okay?"

"Yes, ma'am." He checked the time as he watched her leave the bar. As soon as she was out of sight, he pushed away his beer and stretched his arms above his head. He stood and went over to read a bulletin board by the doors. These remote hotels that mainly catered to foreign travelers were almost like hostels: people putting up notices for travel companions, recommendations for restaurant excursions, notes for guests. It was nice to have a sense of community when you were so far from home. It actually amazed him that visitors were traveling here so soon after the war.

He realized his foot was tapping impatiently, and he checked the time again. Three minutes. He decided to leave it another two minutes so the people in the bar would not notice they'd left together. No one needed gossip in a hotel like this.

As soon as those minutes had passed, he strode to the stairwell. The hotel was situated on just two levels: the main reception floor, where the bar and restaurant was, and the upstairs, where all the rooms were. He passed his own room, checking the handle to make sure it was still locked without breaking stride.

The door to her room was around a corner from his. It was slightly open, yellow light from inside peeking out into the darkened corridor. He tapped his fingertip on the door, half as a knock, and half to push it open. He took a breath to slow his pumping heart as he opened the door.

"Hi," she said from the desk chair. Glasses were perched on her nose as she held the piece of metal up. "Try as I might, I can't find anything special about it."

His eyes were on her tiny frame, dwarfed by the large leather swivel chair that seemed out of place in the otherwise spartan room. Her legs were pulled up beneath her, and her sweatshirt had slipped further, so now her whole shoulder was exposed. It shouldn't have been sexy in and of itself. But he'd never wanted to kiss anything as bad as he wanted his lips on her bare shoulder. *Play it cool, Stanning.*

He moved toward her, and she threw the piece at him. He snatched it out of the air and dragged his eyes from her. As soon as he saw the piece, his attention was arrested, completely, as if Henrietta weren't in the room. It was two pieces of metal, actually, fused together by heat. He'd seen it hundreds of times. An explosion had caused this. He already knew that the part number stamped on one side of one of the pieces identified it as being a part of a C-130 aircraft.

Now the question was, was the explosion an accident, an act of war, or something else? He sat on the bed as he rubbed his thumb over it, trying to think.

"What do you see?" Henrietta asked.

He'd missed her closing the door behind him and pulling the swivel chair toward the bed so she could lean back and prop her feet next to him.

"Nothing good. I'll need to come out to the site with you tomorrow. Something happened to this aircraft, and I need to find out what."

"I thought JPAC was responsible for the location and repatriation of troops' bodies," she said slowly.

"We are. I am." He shook his head, distracted. "That's what I'm here for. You're right. Someone else can find out what happened." He needed to stop trying to solve every problem that came across his path. His commander had drummed that into him when he joined the JPAC team. EOD guys were problem solvers. It was his nature. But it wasn't his job anymore.

A dinging sound came from her desk, and she got up to look at her phone. The light shone around her golden hair like a halo. As she sat to check her e-mails or texts or whatever she was looking at, he closed his eyes briefly to give himself time and space to think of a plan. A plan that wouldn't piss off his commander, or make him feel guilty at not taking action.

Chapter 4

When Harry awoke, she had to take a moment to remember what had happened the night before. An unfamiliar lump weighed down the feeble mattress on one side. Matt. He'd fallen fast asleep in the three minutes she'd been checking her e-mail from the Foundation, so she'd poked him until he slid down to sleep horizontally on the bed. He hadn't woken up, and she'd wondered just how long he'd been awake to cause that kind of deep sleep.

For her part, she'd taken off her sweatshirt and left on a tank, donned sleep shorts, and curled up on the other side of the bed.

She opened her eyes and turned toward him, blinking away the blurriness. He looked so different. At peace. No hint of the player he liked to show. Dark hair cut short around the ears and left slightly longer on top, not short enough to be obviously military, not long enough to look unkempt. A strong chin and cheekbones brought to mind a statue of Apollo she'd helped bring to the surface in the Aegean Sea in Greece a few years back. She wanted to reach out and touch him like she'd wanted to touch the statue. Okay, maybe not exactly in the same way. Scruff darkened his jaw.

His eyes fluttered open, and she saw his muscles tense in his neck. His stare was alert in less than a second. "Henrietta?" he croaked.

"Since we slept together, you should probably call me Harry," she deadpanned.

"We wha—" he began, and then checked his still-clothed body and smiled. "Hell, I thought for a moment we'd had sex and I had no memory of it. What a crime that would be."

"A crime, indeed." Harry smiled back at him. For a second there was silence. Was it awkward that they were in bed, and obviously in the cold hard light of day, he didn't actually want to jump her? She made to get up, but he grabbed on to her arm. She stilled.

"Just where are you going, darlin'?"

Um. "You don't want to get up?"

"Not especially. It's still pretty dark outside, and I have you right where I want you." He winked at her, and she settled back on her side, facing him. "I thought about you a lot since the wedding," he said, turning on his back and stretching before turning back to her. "Did you think about me?"

Every day. "A little, maybe." Her breathing slowed, everything slowed. Ever since she'd met him, she'd fantasized about having sex with him in that garden, what it would have felt like to feel him fill her right there in the rain. This was her time. She was going to have sex with him come hell or high water. She'd been given a second chance. He would be gone soon. She wasn't going to let this opportunity slide.

He held her gaze for a few seconds. "I want you. I want to see you naked. It's all I've thought about. But you need to know that there is no happy ever after for us. I'm leaving in a day or so, and we will probably never see each other again. I just don't want to do anything that will cause you pain, now or later."

Cocky bastard. "Wow, Matt. You're awfully full of yourself aren't you? You think one night"—she looked at the dim light around the edges of the curtains—"*morning*, will rock my world so much that I'll want to spend the rest of my life with you?" She laughed out loud. "I'm sure you're well practiced and all, but still…" She winked at him.

His eyes narrowed. "I *am* going to rock your world, baby." With that he wrapped his arm around her waist and dragged her against him. Instantly her thigh came in contact with something already very hard.

"Are you?" she whispered, a mere inch from his mouth.

His response was a blistering kiss that sent tingles down to her toes. As his tongue forced its way into her mouth, she moaned, and her need for him washed over her like soft wet silt running through her fingers.

"Matt," she whispered as his mouth left hers for her neck, wetly kissing her pulse points that she knew would be jumping against his lips.

He pulled away from her with a frown. "Yes?"

"Take off your clothes." He was still dressed in the clothes he'd come to the bar in the night before.

He jumped up, and eyes still on her, pulled his shirt over his head and unfastened his jeans. Pausing, he said, "And you. I want to see you." He dropped his pants and stood there, all muscles, tattoos, and hard dick. A pool of wetness settled between her legs just at the sight of him. She was going to have him. And he was magnificent.

She stood on the low bed and slowly wriggled her sleep shorts down her legs. She actually saw his dick jump when she revealed that she was wearing no panties. She kicked them off, and without ceremony swiped her tank over her head.

"You are fucking incredible," he breathed as he moved closer to the bed. Her nipples pebbled under his intense gaze. She felt weak suddenly, as if her bones were dissolving. She needed him. Needed his strength.

Matt reached out and touched her collarbone and slowly stroked his hand downward, between her breasts to her stomach where he leaned in to kiss her navel.

She wound her fingers through his short hair and pulled him to her. But he pulled away and scooped her off the bed and into his arms. She was tiny next to him. Delicate, easy to break. And she wanted to feel physically exhausted. Sated. She craved more. She didn't want to be treated like a china doll.

As if he read her mind, he pitched her onto the bed and yanked her legs apart. He licked and kissed his way from her ankles to her thighs, alighting a stream of fire in her. She whimpered for more.

"What do you want, Henrietta? Tell me."

"Make me feel." *Shit. Where had that come from?*

He bit down on her inner thigh, spiking pain and pleasure through her core, making her clitoris tighten and pulse. She'd never felt a need like this before. She gasped. "Oh God, yes."

His fingers bit sharply into her ass cheeks as he lifted her to his mouth. Without ceremony, his tongue was on her clit. Stroking hard and unforgiving. She was so close to coming, she tried to hold on, to prolong the feeling of slipping over the edge. But he plunged a finger deep into her wetness, then two, filling her, stretching her, causing a sliver of pain as his tongue still played on her clitoris. She couldn't hold on any longer. Didn't want to.

She came, fracturing light flickering behind her eyelids as she reveled in the wave that crested in her.

* * *

The sweet, sweet sound of her orgasm echoed in the sparse room. Her tight pussy was still pulsing around his fingers as he slowly withdrew them. He couldn't remember being this hard for anyone before. He needed to be balls-deep in her. Soon.

"Do you have a condom?" she asked.

"I do."

"Thank God," she breathed. "How do you want me?"

"Fast." And hard. He wasn't sure he'd survive anything else. She watched him as he slid on a condom he took from his wallet.

She rolled over and, eyes on him, slowly pulled herself onto all fours. *Fuck me.* She was perfect.

He wasted no time positioning himself behind her. Her blond hair cascaded along her back. He grabbed a hold of his twitching dick and placed it at the entrance to her pussy. Immediately she pushed back, trying to get him inside her. He wrapped one arm around her tiny waist and slowly pushed into her heat. Heat pumped through him as she clenched him inside her. She moaned his name, and right there he almost lost his mind in desire for her.

He pulled out of her slowly, but she didn't allow it. She raised herself slightly, placing her hands on the headboard, and he wished he could see her. See her face, her breasts. He suddenly realized why some people filmed themselves having sex. He'd never seen the attraction before. But now he was totally in favor. If he was only going to fuck her once, he needed a mirror.

He pulled out of her, eliciting a protest from Harry. "Come," he said holding out his hand for hers. "I want to see you so bad." He led her to the old-fashioned dresser in the bedroom. It had a mirror attached to it.

"You are a bad, bad boy." She grinned as she bent from her waist, bracing her arms on the top of the piece of furniture. He now had a perfect view of her face, and breasts. He slid his hand between her legs, closing his eyes as he felt her heavy, hot wetness. She widened her legs in response and moaned as he gently stroked her clit again. His eyes popped open and he watched her facial expression as his fingertips slid around her. Clit, pussy, ass. Just watching her was enough to get him off.

He took his dick in his hand again and guided it into her. It was lighter here than in the bed, and he swallowed hard as he watched himself disappear into her. She was so hot, so tight. Her hair swung down her back with each thrust.

"Harder, fuck me harder," she said, drilling him with her eyes in the mirror.

He held her hips in his hands and drove into her. She met him thrust for thrust. She leaned forward, reached between their legs and touched his balls. She squeezed, and his head just about exploded. Molten lava shot up his spine and back down to his dick as he came.

As he did, she arched her back and her hair fell over one shoulder, showing a tattoo on her upper back. The EOD crest. His old unit.

What the fuck?

Chapter 5

Harry stood up, stretched, and stifled a giggle when Matt groaned as he slid out of her. He hadn't disappointed. Here's to fantasies coming true. She grinned at him in the mirror, but his eyes weren't on her face—they were on her back.

He swept her hair across her shoulders. Ah, he must have seen her tattoo. "It was my husband's unit. EOD," she said, hoping that would be enough information. But no.

"I know what it is, and most of them are divorced. EOD doesn't only stand for Explosive Ordinance Disposal. It also stands for…"

"Every one divorced." She turned to him. "I know. And I'm not divorced."

He stared at her, a rush of different emotions passing over his face. "I'm sorry." He backed away and grabbed his pants. "I know a lot of good guys who aren't here anymore."

"I knew just one." Damn. How had this conversation become so out of control in the space of about thirty seconds? She wished she could dial it back in. Clearly this wasn't a great conversation for him, either; he hadn't looked at her since he said he was sorry.

"It's okay. It's been seven years since he died. I'm fine. Please don't feel sorry for me."

"Seven years? Maybe I knew him. What branch of service?" He was practically dressed now, as if he was layering on armor. She would laugh if he didn't seem so...distressed?

"Air force. Danny McCantry."

His jaw dropped and his head was shaking before he said anything. "Danny's wife was called Marko."

How would he even remember that? Shit and hellfire. This was a whole other kettle of fish. His teeth were actually grinding. She grabbed her shorts and tank and sat next to him on the bed. "My maiden name is Markowitz; Danny and I met when we were twelve. He always called me Marko."

"Danny was my best friend. I just fucked my best friend's wife." He ground the words out, and her heart dropped along with her stomach. Nausea rose, and she took some deep breaths to steady herself. Memories of Danny talking about his unit buddies flooded back. Stories, photos. She'd never met many of them until the funeral. And she barely even remembered the funeral, just the faces of the people that visited afterward.

She touched his arm, but he jumped away as if her hand was white-hot. "Why didn't you tell me?" he said, running his hands through his hair. His voice was low, but it had the intensity of a shout. He grabbed for his clothes and was dressed before she could formulate an adequate response to this nightmare.

"I'm sorry you're upset. This was...unfortunate. But Danny died years ago. I've moved on." Wow, she'd said it so often she nearly believed it herself. Yes, she'd moved on sexually, professionally, and physically, but not emotionally. Never.

"I haven't." He said the two words as two distinct sentences.

"How could you just sleep with me like that? Doesn't Danny's memory mean anything to you?"

Fury flashed through her. Heat throbbed through her head. "How dare you. *How dare you*. Get. Out."

He slammed the door behind him.

Harry curled up on the bed. Hot tears already ran down her face. How dare he judge her? How dare he say the words that only she could say to herself? Damn him. She sniffed and pushed her chin up in defiance, swiping the drips that fell from her face. She wasn't crying for Danny. It was the humiliation. As if someone was calling her out on the doubts she'd always had about the proverbial "moving on" widows were supposed to do.

Damn him to hell. This wasn't her. Why the hell was he getting to her like this? She lived life to the full, every second she could. She knew she would eventually end up with Danny somewhere, so how she lived her life here was completely up to her. She loved life, and she was damn well going to live it the best way she knew how. Adventures, being beholden to no one, and lovely, amazing sex when it felt right.

She wasn't going to apologize for how she lived, how she chose to live, and she wasn't going to let Matt get to her. No way. She got up and turned the shower on.

No effing way.

* * *

What had just happened? What shit had just descended on his world? How was it possible to go from ecstasy to horror in a minute?

He paced up and down his room, trying to make sense of what

had happened. He'd fucked Danny's wife. She'd given herself to him like...like what? his coherent side asked.

Dammit. He'd just basically called her an adulterer. A slut, even. He stopped pacing and fell back on the bed as if he'd been shot. He'd touched her the way Danny had touched her. It was bad. Like he'd broken an unspoken oath.

Danny's death was the faded receipt in the book of his life. There was before, and after. Before, he'd been carefree, light, happy. After he watched his best friend dissolve into the pretty pink mist, he was stressed, tense, heavy. There was light and then dark. Sex served two purposes for him. Got him out of crowds, and for a minute, maybe an hour, made him forget that day.

Suddenly it was as if all his hens had come home to roost. She was right—it had been seven years. He should be over it. But how did anyone get over something like that?

Therapy, a little voice inside said.

He shook his head and ignored the voice. How did he make this better? He couldn't un-fuck her. There was only one thing to do. He would do his job and go back to Hawaii. Forget it happened.

Because he always found it so easy to forget.

Well first he'd have to apologize to her anyway. If she let him. How could this have gone so wrong? It was like fate was playing chicken with him. The odds of meeting her at a wedding, then that amazing—whatever you could call it—in the restaurant garden. Then three months of fantasizing about seeing her completely naked, burying himself in her, only to find her here, halfway across the world, as exciting and beguiling as he remembered. Shit. She had him using words like "beguiling." He was truly fucked. And not in a good way.

Chapter 6

Harry was down for breakfast before anyone else. The metal fragment was back in her pocket, and her work folders were spread out on the big table she'd taken.

"Harry? Harry Markowitz?" An unfamiliar English-accented voice made her look up.

It belonged to an elderly man in a three-piece suit, who looked slightly familiar. Yes, an archaeologist she'd met at a conference maybe three years before.

"Malcolm, right? I'm sorry, I don't remember..." she stood and held out her hand.

He shifted his folders to his left arm and shook it. "Rapson. Malcolm Rapson."

"Of course. You gave a talk on Middle Eastern antiquities. I was transfixed by the artifacts you brought with you. I really enjoyed your lecture." She looked at his folders. Top one was the same as hers. From the Megellin Foundation.

"That's very kind of you to say. Yes. Very kind indeed," he said, already eyeing the breakfast buffet.

"You're here with the Megellin Foundation, too?" Strange that it had more than one surveying team at a time out here. Usually they only worked one area at a time. She flipped over her folder so he could see her identical one.

He looked as puzzled as she was. "How odd, my dear. Where are you working?" He placed his folders on her table and opened the black shiny one and pulled out his map. It was identical to hers in every way, except the highlighted area on his map was geographically to the west of hers, so his east boundary abutted her west boundary. She showed him her map.

"Strange, but not unheard of, my dear. They pay well, so I assume their coffers are not as depleted as some of my clients' are. Maybe they just don't have time to do consecutive surveys."

"I'm sure that's it. Maybe our teams can get together sometime while we're here. I'd love to hear your take on the recent finds near Erbil," she said, trying not to gush. She'd love to spend time with an archaeologist with his reputation. God, if they found something here, maybe she could coauthor a paper with him.

"That would be delightful. We'll organize a get-together later in the week when we've got to grips with the landscape."

"Perfect. Well, enjoy your breakfast!" she said sitting down. What a treat. To be here with a world-renowned archaeologist, one who remembered her name. This was going to be an awesome couple of weeks. And then she remembered Matt, and sighed. Well, once she got rid of him, it would be awesome.

Molly and Jason came down together, making her wonder again if they were already involved. If so, that was unusually fast work for Molly. Usually Molly was a watcher. She'd watch and understand every aspect of a man before she started flirting. She said it was the little things that showed who a man really was. How they talked to waitresses, how they behaved when they thought no one was watching. But she always was.

"Morning, guys. Go grab some food, and we'll make a plan for the day," she said after Molly had kissed her cheek. She swore Molly made her feel more like a mother than she was comfortable with.

A friendly waiter filled three coffee cups with the wonderful aromatic strong brew that made her happy for the morning. She craved it when she wasn't in the Middle East. She hadn't found a restaurant anywhere in the U.S. that made it the way they did here. She looked around briefly and wondered if she could find someone here to give her a lesson. She made a mental note to ask before she left. She inhaled the scent before taking her first sip.

Molly returned to the table and laughed. "You'd think this was the closest you've come to sex in ages by the look on your face. You look like you're in heaven."

Hmmm. "Oh, I am. Taste it and see." She took another sip.

Molly sniffed the coffee and took a sip. A second passed as her face started to flush. She took a quick look around and dribbled it back into the cup.

"Oh my God, are you kidding me?" Harry said, mock sternly. "I'm never going to be able to show my face in here again." She shook her head as if Molly was an exasperating child.

Jason sat next to Molly. "I saw that from over there." He nodded toward the buffet. "I ordered you some tea."

"Thank you, Jason." She turned to Harry. "See, *someone* here has my back."

Harry rolled her eyes. And then she saw Matt. She'd taken the biggest table against the wall, so she had a view of the foyer, but she knew that he couldn't see the others at the table because they were out of his line of sight. She tried to shake her head, but he made a beeline for her nonetheless.

She stood up abruptly, rattling the table and causing the other two to look up quizzically.

"I'm really sorry for what I said. I was so far out of line..." he began.

"Matt, these are my assistants on this trip: Molly and Jason." She pointed around the wall to the guys.

* * *

Fuck.

Smooth, Stanning. Real smooth. "Good morning. I'm Matthew Stanning from JPAC." He shook both of their hands and noticed that Jason looked a little pissed to see him. Competition for the ladies?

"JPAC?" Jason asked, spearing a piece of fruit a little too aggressively.

"Joint POW/MIA Command. It's our job to find and bring our troops home. I was sent to look at the piece you found." He sat down, and a waiter brought him a coffee.

Jason sat back in his chair and crossed his arms. "That was fast, we found it less than twenty-four hours ago."

He wasn't going to explain himself to this pipsqueak. "The air force is just, really, that fast."

Molly leaned over the table, pushing her glasses up her nose as she peered at him. "Ooh, you're air force? How lovely. Did you bring a uniform?"

Out of the corner of his eye, Harry did a double take, and Jason bristled under her words. He didn't know what the fuck dynamic he'd walked into here, but it was interesting, that was for sure. Now if he could just get Harry alone so he could apologize and do his job and move on.

"I do have a uniform with me, yes," he said carefully.

"Is it hard?" Molly continued, making him choke on the coffee he just sipped. There was a silence.

"Is what hard?" he asked, smiling at the sight of Harry with her face in both hands.

"Oh my God, get your minds out of the gutter," Molly said, looking around the table. "I meant, is your job hard? Searching for people you know are dead."

He set his cup back on the table. "It's the most satisfying job I've ever done. It is also hard, for the reason you just said, but when you find them, and you reunite them with their families, who can now give them a proper burial, it's the best job in the world." He looked at Harry. "A close friend of mine died here in Iraq, and we were barely able to bring any of him home. That made me choose this line of work. To bring some peace to people who had always been left wondering."

There was a silence, and then Harry said, "Then I'd like to thank you for your service." In a quiet voice.

"You're welcome." He cleared his throat. "So what are the plans for today? I take it it's okay if I tag along with you?"

"Of course it is," Molly said with a big smile. "The more the merrier."

Matt eyed them all. "You know you're supposed to have security at all times in Iraq, right? All American citizens are."

"We do. We have Mueen. He'll be waiting outside in a truck, ready to take us to the dig," Harry said. "Why don't you grab some food, and we'll gather our stuff and meet you outside in, say, ten minutes?"

Molly and Jason got up and left. Leaving Harry. She looked at him in silence.

"I'm sorry about this morning. I overreacted. I... there was no excuse for it. Just…Danny's still very alive in my mind." He looked back down at his coffee. Damn. He had not meant to say anything as revealing as that.

She got up and pulled out the chair next to him. "He is in mine, too. But I can't live with his memory dictating my every move. I choose to live without him now, because I made the choice long ago to die *with* him."

What? His shock at her words must have reflected in his expression, because she laid her hand on his arm.

"I'm sorry. I didn't explain that at all well." She cleared her throat. "I choose to live without Danny in my head. He was the love of my life. But I'll die with him in my heart. I made my peace with that long ago. You should, too. It's nothing to feel ashamed of, the way you feel. But you can't go through life miserable because of his death."

He scraped his chair on the floor in his rush to get up. People looked up from their breakfast to see who had made the noise. "So we're okay, then?" he asked.

"Of course," she said simply.

He got the hell away from her and took the stairs to the rooms two at a time. This trip was fucking with his head. *She* was. Or maybe it was his own demons, insisting they were heard for once.

Chapter 7

The storm had deposited more sand than usual on the decrepit roads leading to their site, so the ride was slow. And the tension in the truck was palpable.

Everyone seemed to be on edge except Harry, who was suffering only because she could feel everyone else's stress. Mueen wasn't pleased about Matt's presence, although he'd said nothing. He'd just looked at him long and hard, an inscrutable look on his face. He'd looked at him so long, Harry had been forced to clear her throat to dispel the tension.

She didn't know why Jason was so abrupt with Matt, but she planned on talking to him about the level of professionalism she expected when dealing with people outside their team. Molly? She would have to wait until she got her alone to figure out what was going on there.

Meanwhile, they all had to work together if they wanted to complete their job for the Megellin Foundation. The client had to come first because they were the ones who were paying for the team to be there in the first place. All they could reasonably do to accommodate the military presence was use their ground-penetrating radar first, rather than last.

As they got closer to their on-site trailer, Jason and Molly peered out the windshield.

"What the hell?"

Harry squeezed between the seats so she could see what they were talking about. "Oh." The storm had washed sand halfway up the side of their trailer, thankfully the side without the door. But the terrain was now completely different from what they'd photographed the day before. "This happens sometimes, folks. Welcome to the desert." She grinned. This is why desert surveys always had an extra week or so built into their schedule. To allow for the beautiful shifting sands.

"This is an excellent learning opportunity for you two. I'd like you to take more photos today so we can clearly see a before-and-after view on the effect of weather. Jason, in particular, this will be important to your thesis."

Jason nodded and grabbed his camera from behind the seats. As soon as they came to a stop in front of the trailer, he hopped out and clambered onto the roof of the truck to get the same vantage point as he had the day before.

In fact, Harry couldn't believe how dramatically the sands had changed. There was a huge dune in the middle of their sector now. She looked at Matt, inscrutable behind his sunglasses. She wondered how he felt. If he would ever forgive himself for the perceived slight against Danny. She sighed, which prompted him to look at her.

After a second he said, "Do you mind if I go look?" He pointed across the site to the boundary flags.

"Not at all, knock yourself out." She watched him walk methodically around the flags and sighed again.

"You should not have brought him to our door, madam," Mueen said, following her gaze.

It was unusual to even have him speak to her, without his wife present, let alone verbalize an opinion. She turned her full attention to him. "What do you mean?"

"The man. He will disrupt our life here. No good will come from this." Mueen looked at Matt, who was barely visible behind the dune. His accent turned more and more American as he spoke, reminding her that he'd studied at UPenn.

"Anytime outsiders come, our village life is changed in some way." He shook his head. "I sense he will be bad for us."

"Do we disrupt your village life when we come?" she asked. This was her second trip here and the second time Mueen had acted as guard and translator, although the time before, they had to also have three extra armed guards. Thankfully, security could be lighter now. Having four armed guards with military-grade weapons was embarrassing and couldn't have done more to point her out as a foreign woman.

He smiled at her, revealing his perfect teeth. "Yes, of course. But my wife loves you so, that my house is good when you are here."

She laughed. "I love Ain, too."

"She wants you to come to dinner tonight. All of you." He bowed slightly as he offered the invitation.

"We would be delighted. Ain is such a wonderful cook." She was thrilled, actually. Ain was lovely. A ballsy yet demure woman in a man's world. "Is Matt invited, too?"

Mueen looked back at him for a second and laughed softly to himself as Matt appeared to stumble in the sand. "Maybe you should tell him that walking in sand is an art form in itself," he said. "Yes, he may come. I will come for you at six tonight."

"Perfect. Please tell Ain I'm so looking forward to seeing her." Harry had bought some perfumed oils from an aromatherapy store in the U.S. for her and was happy that she could give them to her herself.

Mueen took himself up to the roof of the trailer, and Harry watched Jason and Molly prepare the ground-penetrating radar that would give them, and hopefully Matt, some insight into what lay beneath the surface of the sands here. Although a small worry niggled her; with the shifting sands, they may not get the results they hoped for.

* * *

Just being in the desert brought back memories, good and bad. He tried to concentrate on the job at hand. If this was the scene of an air crash, or at least a crash landing, it was going to be hard to find evidence on the surface. Especially after all this time.

There was an excellent chance that this was nothing but a piece of errant metal, transported here accidentally by who knows what. There'd been so few downed aircraft in Iraq, he was still mystified as to why his commander saw fit to send him here in the first place.

What he needed was to go home. He needed this to be a bust. He just wanted to be out of the sandbox and back on the friendly beaches of Hawaii. He didn't want to get involved with Harry any more than he already had. He blew out a puff of air. In all honesty, Danny would probably piss himself laughing at this scrape he'd gotten himself into. The EOD unit had always had some weird stories of hookups gone bad to entertain each other with. Danny used to say he lived vicariously through their misadventures with women. This was a story for the ages.

He crested the dune and looked around. He saw other people working about half a klick away to the west, and made a mental note to ask Harry about them. There were some old-looking bricks or mortar poking out, the same color as the sand, ruining the otherwise smooth surface of the desert. He checked the compass on his wristwatch and went to the far eastern side of the site. He definitely saw some movement over to the east, too. Busy time of year for archaeology maybe.

When he got back to the trailer he asked about the other teams.

Jason and Molly looked up from what they were doing on a small laptop encased in a steel bounce-proof case. "There are others here?" Molly asked.

Harry squinted at them in the sun. "I ran into Malcolm Rapson at breakfast. He has a team surveying to the west of us. I didn't know about anyone to the east, but knowing Malcolm's here, it wouldn't surprise me. I guess the foundation is just trying to find the best and most archaeologically rich area for the students to dig."

Interesting. Maybe he'd have to check their sites, too. Depending on the velocity a plane was traveling on impact, wreckage could cover more than half a mile. More paperwork. If he found any more evidence, any other metal shards, he'd have to call in a proper team. He couldn't do this alone, and neither should he. They had plenty of experts who would make quick work of this. Not to mention those who liaised with the local government to actually allow them access.

"Fancy private university students. Some of us had to work sites that were absolutely barren of things to learn from," Molly grumbled. "Lucky bastards." She looked around. "Now I really want to plant stuff here to completely confuse them."

"Don't even joke about that. A, I will kill you, and B, karma is a bitch," Harry said. She stood with her hands on her hips, looking like a tiny chief master sergeant. He tried not to smile.

"Don't worry. I wouldn't. I just enjoy fantasizing about it." Molly went back to the machine that looked like a short lawn mower but with probes instead of blades.

"All right, people. Let's get going. You two move on out, and I'll check the feed on the computer as you pass it over the area. Do you have your walkie-talkies?"

"Yes, boss," Jason said, patting his hip.

"I'll call you if I need you to go over anything again. Set up along the western flags, and I'll give you the go ahead when I've had a quick check of the site." She turned to Matt. "Did you see anything interesting out there?"

Nothing as interesting as what is standing in front of me right now. "I saw some old-looking bricks, maybe made out of sand? That's it."

Her eyes lit up, and she virtually bounced. "That's awesome. The storm must have exposed them."

"Come. I'll show you," he said, shoving his hands in his pockets and nodding toward the northeastern side of the dune.

She called Molly and Jason on her walkie-talkie. "Hey, leave the equipment and join us over by the dune. Matt says there's something there."

"Copy that, boss," Jason's tinny voice came through.

Harry and Matt beat the younger two there. "Wow. This is nice. I can't wait to see what these belong to."

Matt was scanning the horizon for other people. Just an instinct probably, and in EOD they learned to always trust instinct over intellect.

Out of the corner of his eye he saw Harry bend over. He

slipped a glance at her denim-clad ass. Dammit all, he was going to hell.

"Hey, moneybags. You dropped these." She stood upright and handed over three one-hundred-dollar bills. He took them. They weren't his. "Are there any more?" he asked evenly.

They both looked around. Matt found one, under a brick. "Can I move this to get this one?"

"That's strange. How did it get under the brick if you dropped them today?"

"They're not mine. I didn't drop them." He fell silent. His mind was running at a hundred miles an hour. Who the hell had money like this, in U.S. currency, to flash around in the middle of the desert? It was trapped under a brick, so it must have been before the storm. By the weathering on the bills, even before. He peered at them closer. They were real. He could tell by the watermark.

"Then who did?"

"They're old. The storm must have somehow brought them to the surface."

Harry bit her lip. "I don't like this. I get heartburn enough thinking about looters, but if anyone finds out about this, this whole site will be a disaster. It'll become too dangerous for us to do anything here."

"Let's not tell anyone. We'll keep it between us. Just us two. That way we can be sure it stays a secret."

Jason and Molly came into sight. Matt stuffed the bills in his pockets.

"Look at the masonry here." Harry pointed to the exposed brickwork.

"Look at the money you're throwing around," Molly said to Matt, holding out a couple more hundred-dollar bills.

Matt hesitated, then took them. "Thanks. Careless of me. Let me know if you find any more."

"Sure we will," Jason said, and with his eyes hidden behind his glasses, Matt couldn't tell if he was being sarcastic or genuine.

After a second, Harry gave more orders. "Okay, as you were. We will circle this area, and all three of us will manage the geophys here so we don't move anything."

"On it," Molly said cheerily as they turned to trudge back over to their equipment.

He and Harry walked back to the trailer in silence. He was definitely worried now. He needed to call this in. The only people moving around this kind of money as far as he knew was the U.S. military or terrorists. Billions of dollars of cold hard cash had gone missing during the war, and although a lot of it had been accounted for, still many millions hadn't. If these serial numbers lined up with that money, Harry, Molly, Jason, and he had just stepped onto an IED. All they could reasonably expect now was the mother of all explosions.

Chapter 8

No more cash was found that day. Thankfully. Harry was perfectly content to have Matt handle that. If indeed there was anything to handle. She suspected that some rich Iraqi had been fast and loose when pulling money out of his pocket in the storm. Although nearly all commerce was done in Iraqi dinars since the allied forces had left.

Anyway, with Matt checking out those bills, she could concentrate on finishing the project and moving on to the next one. Which, if this trip ended on schedule, meant being an extra set of hands on a temple excavation on a beautiful Greek island.

She imagined that for a second. A Greek isle, Matt doing unspeakable things to her on isolated warm sandy beaches. Cocktails in the bar, Matt doing unspeakable things to her in their villa.

She shook her head. She'd be surprised if she would even get him to talk to her about anything other than his mission here, ever again. Of all the unlikely places and ways to meet one of Danny's friends. It beggared belief. *Really.* And he was so hot. It was so unfair.

For all her inner fantasies, a small part of her was devastated for his obvious pain and wanted to help him. Help him move on. But how? Maybe that was just something one had to do by themselves, like she had.

After Danny's death, in retrospect, she'd been too young to know how to deal with the fallout. She'd moved in with his parents, who although well-meaning, tried to make her into their daughter. They insisted on choosing the college she attended and the friends she made, and she was just too young and devastated to fight back. Even when they picked college courses that Danny had planned on doing with his G.I. Bill education benefit.

When she'd finally broken away from their control, she'd changed her name back to Markowitz, a name Danny had always loved. She hadn't been turning her back on Danny when she changed her name, as his parents had claimed, but celebrating the life they had before their very short marriage. Their life before the military.

She shook off the memories and got ready to meet the others downstairs. She wore a maxi dress made of cotton, with long, loose sleeves, and a scarf wrapped around her hair. She swung around in front of the mirror and watched the dress billow out. She almost looked like an Arabian princess, except for the light eyes and hair. *Would Matt like it?*

Damn, must not think about Matt.

She grabbed her bag, the gift for Ain, and locked the door behind her.

Everyone was already there. Matt and Jason sat on opposite sides of the foyer, the latter playing with his phone, and Molly and Mueen were standing chatting at the bottom of the stairs.

"You look lovely," Molly said.

"So do you. I'm not sure I've ever seen you out of pants before," she replied with a smile. It was true. Molly was wearing a long jersey skirt, with a crisp white blouse and a belt that fell low on her hips. Usually she wore jeans and cargo pants cut at various lengths, depending on where they were going. She wondered whose benefit the skirt was for. She hoped Jason's, because the thought of Molly and Matt together made something in her stomach ache.

"Am I late?" she asked Mueen with a little concern. She always messed up the time on her watch when she changed time zones.

"Not at all," he half bowed to her. "Everyone else was quite early."

Harry laughed. "I'm sure Molly's been telling them about Ain's food. I, for one, can't wait!" She looked toward Matt to find him staring at her, expressionless. That nagging in her stomach twitched again, and she wondered if she'd have an ulcer by the time this project was over. She beckoned to him. "Molly, go get Jason. We should get going."

Matt strode to her. All in black he looked like he was ready to smear boot polish on his face and go into the night on a mission. His jacket showed a slight bulge, and she wondered if he was armed.

"Are you okay?" she asked, shoving her arm through his almost forcibly.

He tensed and then relaxed his arm so he could escort her. "I'm starving," he said with a tight smile. She stroked his arm, meaning it to be a friendly gesture, but her fingers scraped his bare wrist, and the heat radiating from his skin made her hand hesitate there. His wrist was thick and strong, and just having skin-on-skin contact, no matter how innocent, scorched her in a very personal way. She felt her whole body drawn to his.

He looked down at her, and she wondered if he'd somehow

felt her body's reaction to him. She snapped her hand away from his and smiled brightly. And then she started to jabber. Badly. "I'm so glad you decided to come. I didn't know if you would. But you can't pass up a chance to taste Ain's cooking. It's divine. I swear if I could, I'd come to Iraq just to eat her food…"

He seemed amused for the first time. He smiled like an indulgent uncle. "Are you okay? Hypoglycemic perhaps?" he asked.

"Oh, shut up," she said. She was pretty sure he laughed under his breath.

"Take a breath, sweetheart. Everything's going to be okay."

She wanted to ask, What? What was going to be okay? The dig? The evening? Their effed-up encounter? But they reached the truck and climbed in. Molly and James sat in the front row, leaving Harry and Matt to slide in the back.

With no air-conditioning, and just the open windows to provide ventilation, it was too noisy and windy to say much. Her thigh was plastered against Matt's on the small seat, although if he closed his legs a little, they'd have their own space. But he didn't. And as they bumped over rocks and holes in the road, he snaked his arm around her shoulders and kept her anchored to him. It was a good job, too. She was so annoyingly tiny that the slightest bump had her whacking her head on the roof of the truck. Another downside to Mueen's truck not having seatbelts.

A frisson of excitement slid through her as he held her to him. Was he merely being chivalrous, or had he forgiven himself? She tentatively laid her hand on his large thigh, half helping her keep her balance over the bumps, and half… not. He didn't seem to notice. *Okay.*

They arrived in good time, the traffic dwindling as they approached Mueen's village. It was really just a small outcrop of brick houses in the middle of nowhere. Last time she came, they'd explained that this was the site of Ain's father's village, and his father's, and as far as Ain could tell, her ancestors' back to biblical times. So families had taken down the old huts, and old houses, and gradually built newer and newer ones. Keeping the tradition of the area, with the amenities of the twenty-first century.

Her last excavation had been twenty-five miles south of the village, and the local sheik had offered Mueen as her bodyguard, along with three other machine-gun-wielding men from another part of the region. Mueen had been the only one who spoke good English. It was lucky for her that this new project was close enough to Mueen that he could guard them again. And even nicer that the security situation had changed sufficiently that only one guard was necessary.

They arrived at the house just as the sun was sending its last rays of the day to illuminate the red tile roof.

Mueen led them in, through several rooms of the house until they were outside again. Cardamom spiced the air, and the scent took Harry right back to two years before, when she was here last. Ain was lighting incense and candles.

"Ain!" Harry said, and then gasped when the slender woman turned around and opened her arms. Though slender from the back, on turning, her belly protruded through her smock. She looked to be around seven months pregnant. "Oh my gosh. Congratulations!" Harry said, claiming her first hug. "Mueen didn't say anything."

"I know, *ma chérie*. I wanted it to be a surprise," Ain said with her delightfully accented English. She'd been educated at the Sorbonne and sometimes lapsed into French, which Harry could just about keep up with. "I'm so happy you could come."

"Wild horses wouldn't have kept us away. I'm thrilled for you. When are you due?"

"In seven weeks. It will be an equinox baby."

Molly interjected. "Oh, Ain. If we'd known you were pregnant, we wouldn't have had you cooking for us, we would have taken you out somewhere."

Her eyes sparkled as Mueen put his arm around her waist. "Exactly. You know my home is my kingdom. I prefer to be in charge here." She batted her eyelashes at Mueen who nodded in acceptance of her words.

"Can you imagine how my life would have been had I told you our news?" He shook his head as if the thought didn't bear thinking about.

Harry loved how Mueen changed when he was with Ain. It was as if he'd found the center of his world. He radiated warmth around her, and it made Harry ache for the same feeling. Except, no. She'd had that feeling before. Once was enough. One love was enough. But that part, the warmth, the familiarity, seemed to be dimming in her memory.

Harry smiled and took a seat on the blankets next to Matt, tucking her legs under her. The terrace was laid out with a fire in a pit away from the structure of the pergola they sat under. Candles flickered around them, and a long colorful blanket lay in front of them. Soon it was filled with plates of *mezza*: marinated pistachios, olives and cheese, hummus, and Ain's specialty of spicy lentils. Everything was served with huge naan breads. Heaven.

Silence fell among them as they dug in. Eyes closed, and appreciative sounds accompanied their first bites. They ate with their fingers, which somehow slowed them down. This was the gift of Middle Eastern eating rituals. It was as if the world had slowed down as they reached for dishes, tore at bread, and sampled different textures and tastes.

A balmy breeze blew in, ruffling Harry's scarf ends. She closed her eyes and tipped her head to feel the breeze.

After five minutes or so, chatter started around her, everyone urging everyone else to try the dishes that were passed to them. Even Jason and Matt seemed relaxed. And with that, the stress fell from her shoulders, too.

* * *

Matt hadn't wanted to go anywhere that night. He was still jet-lagged and soul-heavy from what had happened in the past day and night. But Harry had been anxious to have him attend, and he figured going with them and acting as part of her team would reduce any risk for her, or for him.

The U.S. military wasn't supposed to be in-country, but his commander figured that as long as he wasn't there as a combatant, there would be no harm, no foul by him just checking in on Harry's dig. But Matt wasn't stupid. He was obviously American, and obviously not a business executive, so he thought it best to blend in with the team.

And then he got to sit next to Harry in the truck, and all his logical reasoning went out the window. The first time the truck had hit a pothole, she'd hit her head on the window. He didn't think she'd even noticed or paid too much attention to it. But he did. And he thought he should at least protect her from a road injury. He wrapped his arm around her and clamped her to his side. Protecting. He was protecting her.

Yeah, right.

Her tiny, tight body against his had him desperate to kiss her again. Flashes of her half-naked in the rain, completely naked in the mirror had invaded his brain, and he'd used every counter-measure he knew to keep his dick in check.

He was going to hell. But he couldn't help remembering the feel of her in his arms, naked, brazen. Everything was so wrong in his head.

And then they got to the guard's house. As soon as he stepped inside, the feeling of safety and warmth invaded every suspicious nook in his mind.

The way Mueen and Ain seemed together warmed his black heart. That the universal feeling of love and honor and new life still pervaded this war-torn country, and it made him feel like anything was possible. That war didn't, couldn't, destroy some things.

The food, as promised, was incredible. Especially since his last time in Iraq had seen him eating MREs and whatever the closest airdrop to his firebase had brought. Which had usually been just apples. Ain's lentils were spicy, yet fragrant with herbs and spices, and her bread was fluffy and chewy.

After the feasting was done, he felt very much a spectator as Ain showed Molly how to grind spices, and Mueen played chess with Jason. Harry leaned against the doorjamb with a glass of hot tea, watching in amusement as Mueen kicked Jason's ass with his aggressive moves on the board.

Matt pushed aside a hanging bamboo curtain that led to the garden and stepped out into the cool night. The lights from the small house illuminated the garden. Herbs he recognized and a bunch of stuff he didn't grew in wooden raised beds. Probably where Ain got her seasonings. A raised bed at the end of the enclosure had nothing but flowers along it. A riot of bright jewel-colored blooms covered the whole seven-foot-or-so bed. He was not that into flowers, but even he appreciated the beauty of it. Looked like it took lots of tending to.

In among the stems he saw a small cross. Odd.

He looked back at the house and then peered closer at it. It looked like two sticks of cinnamon tied together. But it was definitely a cross. Not improbable in Iraq, a country with Christians, but he knew this family was Muslim by the prayer mats he'd clocked in their front room as they'd walked through the house. Idly he looked back at the house and then at his watch which had a compass. Yup. The prayer mats had been facing Mecca.

"What are you doing out here?" Harry came up behind him, carrying an extra glass of tea.

He took it and sipped. "Just looking at the plants. They seem to not have any insect enemies here. In my yard these plants would have been eaten in days."

She laughed quietly. "I know nothing about you. I was just surprised you had a yard, but I don't know why. Where do you live?"

He took a relaxing breath as he imagined his house near the beach in its quiet neighborhood. He should be back there by now. Maybe he could leave tomorrow. "Hawaii. You?"

"I have a house in Boston, but I'm rarely there." She turned and looked at the other plants that he'd passed to look at the flowers.

Suddenly he didn't want to be alone with her. Not here, in a garden at night. It reminded him too much of what he'd done to her at the rehearsal dinner. He took a breath, and immediately Danny's face invaded his brain. Laughing, eyes closed as he belly-laughed, and as he always did, he spun out in slow motion, leaving nothing but a pink mist of blood and vaporized body parts.

"Are you okay?" Harry was at his side, hand on his arm, and he had no idea how she got so close.

"I'm fine. Why wouldn't I be?" He struggled to not jump away from her, but instead he moved from her touch slowly, pretending to look at the basil. He shoved his shaking hand in his pants pocket and chugged the rest of the tea with his other.

"You zoned out for a second there." She laughed. "You must be tired still. We'll leave in a little while. Ain was packing up some spices for Molly, and we should grab Jason before he loses his mind."

"Huh? What's wrong with Jason?" What the hell had he missed while he was out in the garden?

"Mueen keeps beating him at chess. Fast and roundly. I left the house just as Jason was failing to find the humor in it." She held her hand out as if she wanted him to take it. "Come on."

He didn't dare touch her again, not with his equilibrium so screwed up. He really hoped that he could get back home tomorrow. He needed away from this clusterfuck of Harry and Iraq. The unlikeliest combination that seemed perfectly created to fuck with his head.

Chapter 9

The journey back to the hotel was slightly tenser than the ride there. What with Jason still smarting at being beaten so easily by Mueen, and Matt glaring out the window, literally on the edge of his seat looking for danger as they slowly bumped back, Harry was certain that the vehicle was emitting a force field of negativity that no one would dare penetrate.

When they eventually got out of Mueen's truck, they gathered around him to shake his hand and thank him for the evening.

"I'll be here at eight for you, as usual," he told them out the window as he peeled away, leaving them in the massive driveway of the hotel. Sometimes he reminded Harry more of an American than an Iraqi. She waved as he left.

"I am going to bed. I'll be down for breakfast at seven as usual," Harry told them, keen to end the evening and at least try to encourage the others to do the same. She'd been on edge since she found the artifact from the military plane and didn't want to invite trouble by having Molly or Jason fool around in the bar or the pool at night. They were pretty close to her age, but she still felt responsible for them.

"Me too," Molly said firmly. "I'll walk with you." She took Harry's arm and steered her toward the entrance.

"Good night, guys." Harry waved over her shoulder, leaving the two moody men behind them.

"Jason is such a piece of work, right?" Molly said as soon as they were through the doors.

"What do you mean? The chess thing?" Harry asked.

"Yes of course the chess thing." She sounded exasperated. "Why is it that men are such poor losers? How can he get angry because someone beat him at a board game? It's ridiculous." Molly was walking faster and faster, clomping up the stairs as she spoke. "It's so juvenile."

Harry thought about Matt's instinctive reaction to her revelation about Danny. Accusing, blaming her. "Yes, they are. They really are."

"I mean, would he do that with his kids?" Molly ploughed along her train of thought, making Harry smile. She had obviously been stewing about it all the way back to the hotel and was just venting. "Would he be angry if his kids beat him at something? Is that, like, abuse or something?"

They reached Harry's room, and she took out her key. "Molly. You're twenty-three and a grad student. So is Jason. You met him three days ago. Please tell me you're not planning on having kids with him already?" She gave Molly a look. A second passed as she watched emotions pass over Molly's face.

"No. *No*. Of course not. But every woman who meets a man wonders what he would be like to marry, to have kids with. Even if it's only for a second. It's normal. Any man you're interested in, that is. It's just something we keep an eye open for, right? It's, like, biology or something." Molly reached in her bag for her keys and made her way to the next room.

"Right," Harry said softly, turning and hiding the frown that she knew was on her face as she opened the door. "G'night."

"Night, Harry."

Did all women think about that? She never had. Never. She sat on the edge of her bed. Seriously? She was supposed to consider every man she liked as a potential parent and husband? And it was biology?

It made sense. All the studies that had been done about being attracted to men who had a symmetrical face or a strong jaw...her mind skipped ahead to Matt. He had both of those things, but she'd never once imagined being married to him, or having kids with him. Was there something wrong with her? Or was Molly wrong?

Molly was young, but Harry knew that she had an IQ of 149 and had rarely scored less than perfect on any standardized test she'd ever taken. And the only reason she knew those things was that Molly'd let it slip when they'd been out drinking in Thailand. If memory served, it had been the Mekong. The liquor that thought it was a nail polish remover. Harry stuck out her tongue in disgust at the mere thought of it.

Urgh, enough of the navel-gazing. She yawned and stretched, got up to lock the bedroom door, and slipped into her sleep shorts and tank again, pausing for a second as she caught a whiff of Matt's soapy scent as she pulled the tank over her head. *Yum.*

She slipped between the sheets and paused for a second. Nope. Still not thinking about having kids with him. Other things, yes. Procreating? Definitely not.

* * *

Matt knew something was off as soon as he stepped in his room. A scent of tobacco, maybe? He closed the door and looked around the room. To the average person, it would look the same as he'd left it. To Matt, it was obvious someone had searched the room.

He wasn't entirely surprised. All through training, they'd always been told that as soon as they were in a foreign country, they were to assume someone was going through their things.

But this was different. This wasn't some provincial policeman curious about what a U.S. serviceman was here for. Or a hotel worker looking for valuables. This was a pro job.

He opened the wardrobe. He'd hung up his uniform and three tan uniform t-shirts, and two uniform blues shirts. He'd hung them in a group of two, then one, then the four other items together. Now they were hanging in one pair and then five together. They'd been careful about the bag he'd placed on the floor but not how the clothes were positioned on the rail.

He opened a drawer in the dresser. He always placed his socks in as if he'd dumped them straight in from the suitcase. A casual observer would assume he was messy. But he also always placed one pair of woolen socks, facing west. W for woolen, W for west. Now they were messed in with the rest of them.

Everything except for those two things were perfect. He couldn't tell if the bag had been touched, although seeing that the searcher was obviously professional, he had to assume so. Luckily he never traveled with anything that could be used against him, or the U.S.

Slowly he turned around, looking at every item of his, and the hotel's. His breath steadied as he surveyed the room. Windows were closed, the blinds were half-down where he'd left them, the bed was made, although God knew he was going to examine that carefully before he got in it. He was looking for one thing, one thing that might tell him exactly why his room had been searched. And then he found it.

In the threadbare carpet there was a slight indentation where a foot of a chair had been. It was slightly to the right of where the chair was now. Clumsy for a pro, but maybe he'd been disturbed. Quietly, he got on his hands and knees and flipped onto his back so he could look under the chair. Somewhere in his fucked-up brain he half expected to see a pressure switch to a bomb, for no good reason except his brain had been messing with him since he'd landed here.

It wasn't a pressure switch, it was a bug. A quarter-sized round bug that looked like a watch battery, smooth and flat. Two tiny antennae poked out of it.

He sighed as he looked at it, relaxing a little. You don't booby-trap a room and bug it at the same time. It was usually one or the other. If his room was going to explode, no one would leave an additional piece of equipment like a bug. Too easy to trace signals.

Sitting up, he wondered. No one knew he was even in country except immigration and his commander. And Nitro. But Nitro was there to guard him. Which reminded him to call him the next day to arrange to see him for a drink. If he was still here, that was.

He leapt up. Shit. He should check on Harry's room, too.

As he let himself out of his room, he called himself out on his excuse to go see her. Who would professionally search the room of an archaeologist? Or bug it, come to that.

By the time he knocked on her door, he'd persuaded himself that it was imperative that he search her room for a matching bug. Vital, even.

The door wrenched open. Harry stood there in the same clothes that had entranced him yesterday. Tiny soft cotton shorts and a tight-fitting tank top. She scrubbed her eyes with her fists. Dammit. Was she freaking crazy? He could have been anyone.

"What the fuck are you doing, opening the door in the middle of the night?" he stormed.

"You knocked." She yawned and stretched her arms over her head, showing off a luscious section of tanned belly. "That's how it works. You knock. I answer."

"And if I'd been a crazed gunman with a grudge against Western women?" He slammed the door behind him.

"Then I'd be dead, and I guess by morning, you'd be feeling guilty because you forgot to warn me that there were crazed gunmen in the hotel." She grinned.

Un-fucking-believable. He took a breath and closed his eyes. He did not want to punch a hole in the wall. That would be bad. Bad. That would be bad. He repeated that in his mind until Harry opened her sassy mouth again.

"I was sleeping. What do you want?"

He paused, remembering why he'd come in the first place. "A good-night kiss." He shrugged and almost laughed at the expression on her face: half disbelief and half annoyance. Ah well.

He grabbed her by the back of her neck and pulled her in. Her eyes were wary, but she said nothing. He angled his head as if he was going to kiss her, and he felt her take a step back. He pressed his lips against her ear and whispered, "My room's bugged. I just want to see if yours is, too."

Harry jerked her head away from him and seemed to search his face. She nodded slowly. And then grinned. He watched perplexed as her hand swung back, almost in slow motion, and then flew forward and slapped him. Not hard, but still.

"What the..." He resisted the temptation to rub his stinging cheek.

Her smile got wider as she spoke. "How dare you. You can't just kiss me, you judgmental oaf." She swept her hands around her and shrugged, giving him the opportunity to look at the stuff in her room.

He circled the room until he got to the huge desk chair she'd been in the night before. "It really wasn't... I really didn't think that." He got on his hands and knees again and looked under the chair. Nothing. Then under the metal casters, next to the wheels. Bingo.

He was elated for a second that he'd found it, and then a cold finger of realization pricked his spine. If they were both bugged, it must be because of the artifact. Unless every freaking room was bugged, but he couldn't imagine that was the case. The bugs were sophisticated, nothing the Iraqis would have access to at this stage in their redevelopment. Putting them in every single room would require a lot of money, and a lot of manpower to listen to the feeds.

He looked at Harry and finally registered that she was making crazy kissing noises. God help him, but he wanted to laugh. He rolled his eyes at her and nodded toward the door.

Once on the other side, Harry looked expectantly at him.

"I don't know. I have no answers now. But it's better, for the benefit of whoever is listening in, to pretend that we don't know they're there. Just try not to say anything about what brought me here, okay?"

She nodded, and then her eyes widened. "Do you think they listened to us... last night?"

He wanted to put her mind at rest, but in all honesty he couldn't. He shrugged. "Maybe? Until I know who's so interested in us, I won't know. I'm going to find an empty room and check it for bugs, just to make sure it's just us."

"The Iraqi couple next door left this morning. I don't think anyone's checked in since," she said, pointing to her left.

He took out his wallet and removed his military ID. Should be easy. Except he couldn't get caught. If he did, all manner of diplomatic issues would arise. Job-threatening ones.

* * *

Seriously? He was just going to break in? She didn't know a whole lot about the justice system here, but she doubted the authorities would look too kindly upon a U.S. military man breaking into a hotel room, albeit an empty one.

"Okay, but I'm coming with you," she said.

"Sure you're not. Get back in your room and just act normally." His face was quite formidable when he was pissed off. Except he had no reason to be.

"Look. If you get caught, and you're with me, I can at least claim it was a mistake, that we mistook this room for mine? You know it makes sense."

He tipped his head and the noise of a crack from his neck startled her. "Okay. But if we get caught, for God's sake, let me do the talking."

What a nerve. "Because you've won over everyone here with your charm and wit?" She shoved her fists into her waist at each side and waited.

"Fair point. Let's get this over with." He leaned against the door and knocked. The weight of his body muffled the sound of the knock. No reply.

Harry looked up and down the corridor, checking for guests or staff wandering around, but it was empty and quiet. She glanced back at Matt, but the door was already open and he had disappeared inside. She made a mental note to make sure she double-locked all her doors around him.

She elbowed the door open and slid in. "You are way too good at that. Did you have a criminal childhood or something?" she whispered.

"Or something." He switched on the small desk lamp and looked around.

She watched as he lowered himself to the floor and looked under the furniture, then peeked out the door to check for unwanted guests. Boots clomped on the stairs, sending her heart rate into the stratosphere. "Someone's coming," she hissed.

Matt was lying on the floor looking up at the desk. "Close the door and flip the light switch," he said.

She did as she was told. Footsteps went to the far end of the corridor and inexplicably came back. Oh God, was it the security man? She backed away from the door silently. Up and down the man paced. She got on her hands and knees and crawled in the dark over to Matt so she wouldn't make a noise. "He might be there all night," she whispered as she approached.

Suddenly her hand was on his leg. His big, hard leg. They both went completely still. "Sorry," she said pulling away and sitting with her back to the bed, propping her feet against his legs. "Any ideas?"

"There were no bugs in here, so best guess is that we were the target. I'm going to have to call my commander to update him."

Harry began to worry. What if his commander insisted he leave? What would she do then? Would she be safe? "Can you… not call him?" she asked in a whisper.

"Why?"

"I'm worried he might make you leave." Urgh, why did she say that?

She felt his leg shaking against her foot. Was he...? "Are you *laughing* at me?"

"Pretty much," he managed. He cleared his throat softly. "You were itching for me to leave a few hours ago, weren't you? Admit it. I could see you planning the rest of your work once I'd gone."

No point trying to deny that one. "That was before I knew we'd been bugged."

"Look, sweetheart. I'm not an accountant. My boss isn't going to snatch me away at the first sign of trouble. I'm military. He's going to want me to stay until I figure out what's going on. He may even send backup. So I'm not going anywhere."

"Just so you know, I'm not scared for myself, but for my grad students, and Mueen and Ain. I can't protect them myself if these bugs were placed by someone with nefarious intentions." That much was true. She was never scared of trouble for herself.

"Nefarious?" She swore his leg started shaking again. "You sound like a woman in those Agatha Christie books. Wasn't there a *Murder in Mesopotamia* or something?"

"Let's not talk about murder, okay?" She wanted to talk out her thoughts, though. "The only good reason to bug my room would be to find out if we'd discovered anything from our archaeological survey. The only reason to bug you is to find out something military. The only reason to bug us both is to find out about that damn plane part, right?"

He shifted his legs away from her and sat up, his voice much closer. "That's impressive deduction. I had come to the same con-clusion. Who did you tell?"

She thought. "Molly and Jason know, but if they told anyone, their career would be over, so they know better than to men-tion it. Sadie knows about it. As does whoever gave you orders to come here. As far as I know, that's it. What about you? Who did you tell?"

"No one. My commander knows, and that's it, as far as I know." He sighed heavily.

"What's the matter? I mean, apart from the fact that we're sitting in the dark avoiding a security guard and our rooms have been bugged?"

"I don't know. Someone, somewhere knows something about that piece of metal. Which means it is significant in some way. I'm frankly scared to contemplate that possibility."

Harry shivered. She did not like it a bit that Matt, of all people, was scared. "Why?"

He shifted to his feet and took her hand and pulled her up, too. "I think the guard has gone."

His hand was warm and dry. She had a terrible urge to have his arms around her, to have him protect her. But she released his hand. She didn't want to mess with his head. She didn't want the discussions about Danny that would invariably follow.

"Why are you scared that someone thinks the metal is significant?" she insisted.

He checked the door for sound and then opened it, holding it and nudging her back out into the corridor. "Can we talk about it tomorrow? Maybe at the site, where no one can easily overhear us?"

She shrugged. Fair enough. She wasn't that interested in talking about it anywhere anyone could overhear. "Sure." She opened the door to her room. "Good night."

"Good night," he echoed.

She shut the door behind her, slipped the deadbolt, and for good measure, placed the trash can next to the door. It wouldn't stop anyone from coming in, but it would certainly alert her to the fact that she was about to die.

Dramatic much?

She climbed into bed and turned off the light. Thoughts ran through her mind. The lovely idea that her next job could be in Greece had become more and more remote as the day had passed. The idea that light and carefree sex with Matt would be anything even approximating light and carefree also faded. The past twenty-four hours had been a perfect storm of her past and present colliding with her work.

She got up and put a night-light on. She doubted even that would keep her nightmares away tonight.

Chapter 10

By the time his alarm went off, Matt had gotten no more than a couple of hours of sleep. His eyes felt like the time he'd been caught in a sandstorm in Afghanistan. Gritty and sore.

He'd spent some of the night outside on his small balcony talking with his boss on the phone. With the doors closed so the bug wouldn't pick up his conversation, and the moon bright enough to see anyone below, Commander Jenks had been initially happy to hear from him. But as the conversation went on, and Matt filled him in on the hundred-dollar bills and the bugs, he'd grown quieter.

Matt understood why. It was a clusterfuck. He'd been in Iraq for twenty-four hours and there was no bright side to the situation, and they both knew it. Jenks didn't have to explain his quietness. What could he say?

That he couldn't leave these three American citizens in danger? That the news was obviously out that an airplane had had some kind of malfunction and probably crashed? That someone had put that together with the fact that there was no record of a plane being lost and figured out what Matt had as soon as he'd seen the money flapping in the breeze?

The bugs just added another nail to the coffin. If anyone else even thought there may be millions of cold hard cash under the sand, well, some people would do anything to get their hands on it. Anything.

He had to tell Harry, but he needed to touch base with Nitro and get some level of support. If he'd been contracted to provide in-country security, well, they needed a shit ton of it now.

He checked his watch again, and no, he couldn't get an extra thirty minutes of shut-eye. And frankly he didn't want to leave Harry unprotected. Nitro tonight, then, after he spent the day glued to Harry's side. This was his mission. This was how he'd make it up to the karma gods for having sex with her. He would protect her. For Danny.

Danny's face floated in his head again, and he dug his short nails into his palms to hold back the next image. It was no good. The explosion came as it had always done. But this time he flinched at the *boom*, felt the heat of the desert against his face as the dirt settled. They'd all fallen backward at the explosion, and not for the first time. Usually they all lay back laughing after someone had fucked up a controlled explosion. But not this time. He sat there, dirt and blood in his mouth, deafened. His best friend's torso had disappeared.

More bangs. He shook his head, dry dirt flying from his helmet. Except it didn't. The noise dissipated, and he realized where he was.

Jesus. How was is possible that he was getting worse with time instead of better? It must be being in Iraq that was setting him off. He sat carefully on the bed and dropped his head into his hands, rubbing the back of his longer than usual hair. He needed help. In every way.

But not now. Now, he had a mission.

He made short work of his shower, electing not to shave in order to blend in as much as he could. He put on his jeans, a t-shirt, and an open-collared shirt that he figured would see him through the day. He gave a passing thought to getting laundry done while he was here, given his minimal luggage, and headed downstairs to breakfast.

Keep it together. Just keep your head together for another couple of days.

Harry and her "kids" were already eating, and he nodded at them as he made his way to the buffet at the back. He heaped food onto his plate, not really paying attention to what he was choosing, and grabbed the chair at the end of their table.

He started to chow down and noticed the silence at the table. He slowly looked up. All three of them were looking at his plate in awe.

"Are you…hungry, by chance?" Molly said with a grin.

All of their plates had one piece of fruit and one piece of bread on them. His basically had one of everything from the buffet on it.

Swallowing, he leaned back in his chair. "I'm used to eating when I can so it doesn't matter if I'm stuck somewhere with no food later. Sorry." He grinned back at them.

"Well, you don't have to worry about that here. I make sure all my workers are well fed. When we spend a whole day at the site, the hotel sends food for us," Harry said, taking a sip of her coffee.

"I'm not one of your workers," he replied, spearing a section of orange and shoving it in his mouth. Somehow Ain's food had made him hungry. Really hungry.

"That's what you think," Harry said with a raised eyebrow.

"It's only fair, dude," Molly said. "I mean, you're a big, strapping man, if there's equipment to lug—"

"And there's always equipment to lug," Jason interrupted.

"—then it's not very chivalrous of you to be there not helping." Molly actually batted her eyelashes at him.

He choked back a laugh, and inhaled a morsel of bread. Harry hit him on the back, a little too hard to be a genuine offer of help. He eyed her. "You done, or you want to beat on me some more? Anything you want to say?"

"I'm good. Eat up, airman, we leave in ten." She sat back down and opened her black file.

He continued to eat, and as he looked around at the other guests, he clocked an older man, also looking at the same black file. "Is that…?" He'd forgotten the man's name.

"Malcolm Rapson. Yes. Also being funded by the same foundation." He noticed a small frown flick across her face. "Actually, I need to speak to him." She got up and went over to the man's table.

"It's a little mutual admiration society there," Jason said. This time there was a frown from Molly at his words. But he continued. "It's an occupational hazard of academia. Everyone jockeys position to write papers with each other." Jason's eyes followed Harry in a way that made Matt take notice.

"Although I predict that we find absolutely nothing here. Complete waste of time. There are no records that would suggest anything of interest was ever in this part of the region. It's crazy that one foundation would want to survey such a big area of barren desert."

Matt kept his face impassive, but it was indeed a good question. A hard, cold, solid mass grew in his stomach. The pieces of the puzzle didn't fit together yet, but they definitely belonged on the same table. He tried not to look at Harry, but hell, she was bending over the table that Rapson was sitting at. How could he not visualize her face in the mirror the last time he'd seen her in that position? Dammit. He shifted in his seat to discourage his dick from getting a word in.

No. Just no.

* * *

"How was yesterday?" Harry asked Malcolm as she approached his table.

He looked up and smiled. "Oh, quite average. You?"

She laughed. "About the same. I suspect my grad students will be pretty bored by the end, but it's good experience for them, I guess."

"Agreed. I can't imagine that we will find anything here. I wonder why Megellin thought this was a good place to look for promising excavation areas." He took off his glasses, folded them, and then scratched the side of his head with them. "The only reason I can think of is...No. Maybe I've watched too many movies." He chuckled. "Indiana Jones has a lot to answer for, I'm afraid."

"May I?" she asked, pointing at the chair.

"Oh, my dear, of course, I'm sorry. Forgive me for being rude." He got up and pulled out the chair, waiting until she was seated before he sat back down.

"It was *The Mummy* movie for me," she whispered, delighted at his humor. "So what did Indiana Jones make you think we were here for?"

"If you excuse the melodrama, there is a remote possibility that we are actually looking for something that Megellin wants to find. What do you think about that?" His eyes seemed to sparkle at the suggestion of intrigue. "What do you know about the foundation?" he continued.

Surprised, she took a second to answer. "Not much. I know they sponsor university digs, they can pull strings to get visas to countries, and they never seem short of money. I did a survey for them a couple of years ago in Kurdistan. Uncovered a burial ground that a team from Amersham College later excavated."

"Amersham, you say?" He nodded sagely. "Ah well, it's probably nothing." He leaned forward conspiratorially. "I have some feelers out, my dear. I'm expecting some return calls later today."

"Well, actually, I came by to ask if you wanted to have dinner tonight for some industry chat?" She was actually thrilled that he was so engaging. A lot of scholars in her field were standoffish. Especially the English ones. And besides, she wanted to figure out if she needed to warn Malcolm, too. If his team found anything like they had on their site, she'd have to warn him about the bugs.

"I'd be delighted, my dear. You did hear about what happened on the last night of the Ancient Bronzes conference in Istanbul this past September, didn't you?" He got up with a wink.

The wily old gossip! "I can't wait to hear about it." She smiled.

They agreed to meet that evening in the lobby before he left. Harry returned to her table. "Guess who has a dinner date tonight?" She said as she grabbed her now lukewarm coffee and plunked back on her chair.

"Do we need to try to find you some condoms?" Molly said, elbowing her in the ribs.

Harry rolled her eyes in response. "Are we ready to head out?" And then she tried to remember if Matt had used a condom. She thought he had, but... Was that something she could ask him?

Her mind went to that night, and she couldn't help but look at him. He'd been silent since she returned to the table. His expression was completely inscrutable. God, he was so handsome. She wanted to twine her fingers through his hair, which she was sure was longer than regulation. A heat spread through her as she thought about that stubble scratching her skin. She squeezed her thighs together and felt a flush sneaking up her face. His eyes hadn't left hers.

Okay, nothing to see here, move along. She jumped up. "Are you coming to the site with us, or do you have other things to do?" she asked him.

"I'm with you. I'd like to keep my eye on you all. If that's okay?" he replied, also getting up.

In truth she was relieved. She'd always felt safe in Iraq, but not now, not with a bug in her room. Not with the stupid, *stupid* piece of metal they'd found. She didn't feel afraid exactly, just wary. She had no doubt in Mueen's ability to protect them if necessary.

Initially she'd been unsure of the man the sheik had picked to protect them on their first visit; she'd assumed that he'd been chosen because he spoke perfect English. But she'd once seen him fieldstrip his weapon and put it back together again. Silently and in just a few seconds. She'd been so amazed by what she'd seen that she stayed hidden and watched him do it over and over until she'd realized that he was doing it with his eyes closed. After that, she'd been 100 percent sure that they were safe with him. She wondered if they needed to tell him what they'd found.

She knew the answer. It was yes. They should tell him. And she knew that Matt wouldn't be happy with that. But she intended to ask the question nonetheless. She held up her hand to him and waited for Jason and Molly to disappear into the lobby.

"We need to talk about when we can tell everyone about the bugs, about what you think the metal could be. Mueen, Molly, and Jason have a right to know," she said in a low voice.

He took a second and looked out the window of the restaurant. She couldn't tell if he was looking at something or considering his response.

"Go to the site. As soon as you've left, I'll check Molly's and Jason's rooms for bugs. If they are not bugged, there is no reason to involve them right now. And if we don't involve them, then we don't need to involve Mueen, especially since he's…"

She fisted her hands. "He's what?" she virtually hissed at him. "The enemy? Iraqi? How could you say that about him after you enjoyed his hospitality last night?"

"Calm down, cupcake. I didn't say that. I meant, there is something that bothers me about him." He held up his hands to ward off the barrage of aggression she'd opened her mouth to fling at him. "His English is too good. His weapon is perfectly placed on his body. Nearly everyone here slings their gun around their shoulder like a purse, but not him. I just… don't know what to make of him. Yet."

Harry took a breath. Okay, fair enough. "I'll tell you something if you promise not to blow up," she said.

Now it was his turn to look pissed. "What?"

"Promise?"

"I. Promise," he bit out.

"I think he used to be in the Iraqi army."

Chapter 11

He was there when we found the piece of wreckage, or whatever it was, and he knew I was calling the U.S. military about it. He knows that's why you're here, and he hasn't told anyone, has he?"

"He's an Iraqi *soldier*? Did you double-check that it wasn't him, or one of his friends that *set the bomb that killed your husband*?" He grabbed her arms and squeezed.

"Let go of me, that hurts," she said, looking pointedly at his hands. He dropped them immediately and stepped away. His eyes said sorry, the rest of him, not so much. He turned and walked a few paces in the now deserted dining room. He paced back to her, opened his mouth as if to speak, then clamped it shut and paced away again.

When he headed back to her, she held out her hand to stop him. "I said, I *think* he might have been. I don't know. But I do trust him. I trust him with our lives," she said simply.

"Well, that makes one of us."

She shrugged. "There's not much I can do about that except ask you to trust me." *Please don't mention Danny's trust. Please.*

He paused, frowning at her words. But as if he'd heard her silent plea, he just shook his head. "I'll see you at the site. I'll be about thirty minutes behind you."

Molly was hanging out of Mueen's truck door, looking for her. She pulled her ubiquitous scarf up over her hair and pushed through the hotel doors. A waft of dry hot air hit her, and it lifted her spirit a little. She loved the climate here. If only she could get Matt off the ledge he seemed to be perpetually on, maybe he'd see something here beyond the country he was at war with. And maybe not.

"What are we wasting our time on today, boss?" Jason asked.

What? "Excuse me?" she said.

Molly looked back from the front seat with a frown.

"Well, it's clear we're not going to find anything here. Why don't we pack up, write that report, and go home? I spoke to the girl on Rapson's team."

Now Molly really turned around in her seat, and the two women eyed each other.

"And?"

"They have tentative plans to leave tomorrow. They think it's a bust." He smiled smugly. "I do, too. I mean Rapson has a more… experienced team, so they should know, right?"

Wow. Maybe she'd made a huge mistake hiring him for this contract. There probably wasn't a maybe about it. Thank God he was a freelancer.

"Firstly, the 'girl' you spoke with is not a girl. If she's working for Rapson, I'm fairly sure she's a woman. Secondly, you don't work on Rapson's team, you're on my team. If you want to see if he will take you on, then you are free to do that. But we will fulfill the contract I signed as planned. We have at least one more day of geo-phys to do, and one day of report preparation. And that's assuming we don't find anything. But again, Molly and I have worked bigger sites than this by ourselves, so if you don't want to be here, you can go. No hard feelings."

His eyes flicked to Molly as if for support, but her eyes were covered with her big sunglasses, and her expression was difficult to define. She certainly didn't say anything in his support, and for that, Harry was grateful. She wondered if it was a gender thing. Maybe he valued Professor Rapson's opinion over hers. She mentally shrugged. He was entitled to think what he wanted.

"I...didn't mean anything by it. I was just saying what that g— that wo— what Katherine had said."

Harry hid a smile. "Okay," she said mildly and looked out of the window as if she'd never seen the desert before.

As soon as they arrived at the site, Jason jumped out, and without being asked, for the first time, started prepping the ground-penetrating radar and the laptop that read its results. Mueen climbed nimbly onto the roof of their trailer and settled in for the day again.

Molly exchanged a big grin with Harry as she lugged a cooler filled with ice and water into the trailer. Maybe Molly wasn't so interested in Jason. Certainly the tide of opinion seemed to have turned since his epic loss at chess. Maybe they were only just now seeing everything in him that a résumé couldn't reasonably tell them.

* * *

Matt let himself into Molly's room first. She'd left her laptop and phone on the desk in a devastatingly huge display of disregard. The locks were truly so flimsy that he was amazed they were still there. Still, now he couldn't tell her to put them away.

He checked under the desk chair for a bug and found nothing. He looked at the rotary phone that was on the desk but figured someone as young as Molly probably wouldn't even consider using it. He knew that practically every hotel phone in Iraq was bugged anyway. Whether anyone still listened after Hussein was deposed was a different question.

He sighed. What he really wanted was to be taking a morning swim in the Pacific by his house. Fate was cruel. That was sure. He needed help. Professional help. The help he'd been brushing off for seven years. He knew that now. Maybe if he'd taken it when it was offered back then, he would be fixed by now. He was fucked up beyond all recognition. He knew this was true because he still wanted her. Still wanted to possess her even though she belonged to Danny. He couldn't even look at her without wanting to be inside her again. It was like a drug.

A drug with nasty side effects. Flashbacks. Guilt. The feeling that he was no longer in control of his battle-scarred thoughts and memories. It was a control he'd fought hard for over the years, and it was evaporating like clouds in the desert. He took a breath and dragged himself back to the task at hand.

Even the smell of Molly's perfume in the room, and the copious amount of red and black lacy underwear on the floor didn't give him pause. Didn't even make him visualize her in it, not even for a second. Maybe it would take a shrink to get both Harry and Danny out of his head. Maybe everything out of his head.

He was deeply, deeply fucked up.

There was nothing suspicious in Molly's room, so he quietly let himself out and found Jason's.

At least there was no underwear on the floor. Matt checked the desk chair, and all around the table in case, but found no bugs. That was a huge relief. He wouldn't have to argue with Harry about keeping everything need-to-know for now.

He let himself out and made his way back down to the lobby, where he planned on asking them to arrange a taxi for him. As he rounded the corner of the staircase, he literally bumped into Nitro.

"Dude," Matt said as he grasped the banister to stop them both falling. "You are a hazard to be around."

"Sorry, man. I was coming to see you. Keeping my ear to the ground, you know." He paused, then shrugged. "Thought I'd touch base, see if you needed anything." He turned around on the stairs and continued down with Matt, but not before he cast one last look up the staircase. It was a strange look, and Matt wondered if he'd in fact interrupted a liaison with someone in the hotel. Horny bastard. At least that hadn't changed.

"I could use a ride. Is that in your remit?" Matt asked, only half-facetiously. Military contracting firms, although populated with ex-military, usually had very different rules of engagement, and what might seem a logical request for someone who was contracted to be his security point man, chauffeuring might not count.

"Anything you want, buddy. I'm here for you. Just keep me in the loop, and I can anticipate what you might need."

David "Nitro" Church held the door to his Suburban open and Matt got into the passenger seat. As David walked around the back of the car to get in, Matt marveled at the equipment that was installed in the SUV. He was surprised, but also not, to find a military-grade GPS, a handgun Velcroed under the dash so just the butt was showing, and a satellite uplink, for what he couldn't fathom. But he did know contractors, and they did like their toys.

The last time Matt had been in a war zone, he'd been in a

Humvee with only a radio, and it had always been a bit hit-or-miss whether it'd work. In the world of military contractors, money talked.

When Nitro settled in and put the car in gear, Matt asked him about his work with MGL Security. "How long have you been in-country?"

"Nearly a year. Wait. No, yeah, just about a year at the end of the month." David nodded to himself. "It's a long time to be away from home, but it's nowhere near the hardship of our deployments. I have an Internet connection anywhere I am, and a sat phone that works so much better than the ones we had in Afghanistan. You remember those? Jay-sus. It's a miracle any of us got outta there alive."

Matt laughed. "You just never knew how to use it. You thought shaking it like an Etch A Sketch would reset it."

David laughed.

"You enjoy it?"

"Hell yeah. I get paid triple the salary I pulled in the air force. It's not as easy as being in. The politics are worse, believe it or not."

"Ah. There are politics everywhere."

"So what are you really here for, Boomer?" David asked abruptly. "I heard rumors that you'd given up combat. But instead of going to a civilian bomb squad you went…to find dead people?" He sounded skeptical, and when he put it baldly like that, he could see what he meant.

"Yeah." He couldn't count the ways in which he didn't want to talk about this, especially not to Nitro. Especially not sober. "Hey, maybe we'll save the soul-searching until we're better lubricated?"

"Deal. Tonight? Your hotel has about the only bar in a

fifty-mile radius, apart from my hotel. And I'm sick of that bar. Say, eight? We have a good few years to catch up on."

"Yes, we do." Matt agreed.

"Here we are," David said as they skidded to a halt on a sandy path. "I'm not going further; this has a ton of bulletproof shit on it—if it gets caught in the sand, we are never getting it out. And I'm not having it taken out of my paycheck. You can walk the rest."

"Really?" he said, undoing his seatbelt. "Well if I get shot walking from here to there"—he pointed at Harry's ops center trailer—"you better not get a fucking bonus this year."

David's constant smile faded as he took off his shades.

"I'm kidding, bud," Matt said.

"No. Look. That's…no, that's not…it can't be, right?" His voice started to get high-pitched and wobbly. "It's just the desert, right? A mirage? The country's fucking with us right?" He looked at Matt. "You don't see her, right?"

Matt's heart sank as he realized that Nitro had just seen Harry walking toward them. "We're not in a *Tom and Jerry* cartoon, dude. No chick is going to arrive in a grass skirt with a cocktail in a pineapple skin."

For the first time ever, Nitro looked terrified, white and sweating, like he really had seen a ghost.

"It's me, right? This is my punishment?"

"Punishment for what? Pull yourself together, man. That's Harry, Danny's wife. She's an archaeologist. She's really here. Come on. Get ahold of yourself. You don't want her to see you having a fit of the vapors, do you?"

Matt watched as David slowly pulled himself together. Matt obviously wasn't the only fucked-up member of the team, then. For a second he wondered about the other four guys who usually deployed in their rotation. Justin, Liam, Bill, and Mark. Maybe there wasn't anything unusual about his own flashbacks after all. Maybe they were all messed up.

Harry stood in front of the truck waiting for him to get out. He stole a look at David. How well did he know her? Or had he met her before Danny died? David reached for the interior door handle and opened the door. Matt got out, too.

"Harry, this is David Church. He was…" Matt began.

"Yes, I know. David? I know you were kind enough to come to the house after Danny died; I recognize your face, but not your name. It was all a bit of a blur. You played ball with Danny's little sister when you visited. Thank you for that. Thank you for visiting. And it's nice to meet you again."

He watched them shake hands, smiling, but his brain was whirring in a bad direction. He hadn't thought to visit Harry. Okay, that was a lie. He had thought about going around to pay his respects to Danny's family, but he hadn't. He'd worried that some big guy coming around and breaking down in front of them wouldn't do them any favors. And by the time Danny's death became "normal" inside his head, it was really too late to make a courtesy call.

"What are you doing back here in Iraq? Did you know you'd both be here?" She looked between them with a smile that faltered as neither of them spoke.

David stepped toward her. "Not until I got the wire asking me to meet him at the airport, and since he nearly decked me in the arrivals lounge, I suspect he wasn't expecting to see me, either."

"Wow. So this is all one happy coincidence. I feel like I brought the team back together." Harry grinned.

David slid seamlessly into flirt mode. "If you're not doing anything later…"

"She is." Matt hoped his tone drew a line under that particular thought process.

Harry laughed out loud. "I do have a dinner planned with a colleague. But thank you. Maybe some other time." She looked at Matt and shook her head. "I'm heading back."

Matt hitched his backpack to his shoulder. "See you tonight, Nitro."

"Later, man," he replied as he got back in the Suburban.

"This is turning into a very weird trip," Harry said as they started along the sandy pathway.

"No kidding," he said. "Who are all the extra people?" He nodded toward the trailer, where Mueen was perched. There were about twenty additional people there.

"In all the excitement, I forgot to advise the sheik that our schedule had changed, so he sent a bunch of workers from the area to help out. Generally he chooses the families who need the work and money the most, so I don't want to send them back without anything. So come hell or high water, we will pay them for their day here, even if some of the workers are just kids who will be drawing with Molly for most of the day."

He watched the men all turn at the same time and stare at him. The ones who were crouching stood. Vulnerability prickled at the base of his spine as he fought with himself not to reach for the weapon tucked into his waistband or to look around to see if Nitro was within hailing distance.

Flickering images at the back of his mind battled for head space. Visions of Iraqi soldiers overrunning their position in Basra. Determined young faces with guns as big as their torsos.

Dead faces, blood and red sand.

Chapter 12

Harry stopped in her tracks. "Are you all right? Are you *all right*?"

What was wrong with him? He'd stopped in his tracks and was staring at the young men who had stood up when she had returned to the site.

"Matt." She turned her back to the workers and took his hand, trying to urge a response from him. "What is it?"

His Adam's apple bobbed as he blinked and met her gaze. "Who are they?"

"My workers. We just...We just spoke about that, Matt." Her stomach clenched. What was going on? "Here. Have some water."

He took the bottle and swigged. She watched his chest heave slowly, as if he was struggling for control.

"You're scaring me. Are you okay? Do you want me to get someone to take you back to the hotel?"

"I'm fine," he ground out in a voice that was anything but. He cleared his throat and looked at the bottle in his hand. He screwed the cap and handed it back to her. "Just the heat. I'm fine.

"So who cleared them to work for you?" he asked, nodding at the men who had gone back to their duties.

"This is a dig. No one has to clear them. They work for the sheik. And any antiquities we find here belong to him, so if he trusts them, then I do, too." She swiveled her head toward them, trying to see what Matt was seeing.

"That's not good enough. Not now," he said as if the matter had been settled.

"It is good enough. I won't put up with you interfering in my dig. Period." If he hadn't been so shaky a minute before, she would have been much more…vehement.

"There's no need to get snitty. I'm just trying to keep you safe," Matt said.

She needed to nip this in the bud. "Let's get some things straight. First, it's not your job to keep me safe. It's Mueen's job to keep us safe. Second, my workers are my concern. They are poor local people who desperately need the money that foreign archaeological digs bring to the area. They are hardworking, dedicated, and friendly. I simply won't put up with you scaring them, scowling at them, or doing anything to make them think they are threatened. Trust me, they've had enough fear for a few lifetimes."

She stood with her hands on her hips hoping that he would get how serious she was being. The first time she came to Iraq after the war, the people were so welcoming, and kind. She gradually came to understand that Iraqis don't judge people based on their country, religion, or looks. They judge people on the way they behave. Quite rightly. They never blamed her, or even looked at her funny, because she was American, even though blown-up vehicles and tanks still littered the highways between check-points. There was no way she was going to let Matt treat them in any other way than as hard workers.

Matt said nothing; she couldn't tell if he was looking at her or the workers over her shoulder because of the sunglasses he'd just put on. "Are we clear?"

"Yes, ma'am," he replied almost mildly. "But I resent you thinking I would mistrust people because of their nationality. I mistrust everyone equally." He walked around her and took off toward the trailer.

She scurried to keep up. "Did you find bugs in their rooms?"

"Nope. So let's keep this quiet for now, okay? It could be nothing."

Yeah, right. That's why he's all antsy. A finger of trepidation scurried up her back. She wanted to get through this dig, then head off to Greece. She hoped and prayed that nothing would come of this. The money, the plane part. But frankly, the more she thought about it, the more logical it seemed that there was something unusual about this dig. *Gah!*

"Your workers are about twelve," Matt said evenly.

"I know. Life is different here. The older adults are usually unable to work. Don't worry, we look after them well. We feed them, let them play in the trailer a bit, and the sheik pays the family for their work. However, today, because we're not doing any surface work, they're kind of doing whatever they want for a while. A couple are being taught how to use the ground-penetrating radar, which will be super useful for other digs that might come to the area."

"Who are you digging here for again?" he asked.

"The Megellin Foundation. I've surveyed for them before."

"You just figure out if there's anything interesting here, and then if there is, they bring a team of students to excavate?" he asked.

"Mostly. Sometimes they bring the students even if there's nothing here. It's a good exercise. Not every dig works out. They should get used to that early on in their careers. I did," she said casting her mind back to fruitless digs. She wondered why he was curious about it, but she felt she couldn't ask him without sounding suspicious. She sighed. He was hard work…sometimes at least.

Not all the time, though. Sometimes he was easy. She took a deep breath and blew cool air up her face. It was pretty hard not to see him and visualize him naked. High semi-sleeve tattoos on his upper arms, either side of his torso, and across his back, covering, yet showing, the muscles beneath. She really wanted to take time to look at all of them. She wondered if she'd ever get that opportunity again. He seemed…convinced it was a bad idea. He was probably right.

Molly looked up from the little laptop that deciphered the images sent back by the GPR. "Jason has walked the perimeter on the west side. Nothing unusual so far."

"Can you get him back for a minute? I'm going to fast-track this. I'd like to intersect the site diagonally in a cross pattern, to get a general idea of the layout down there, if there is one. Then we'll examine areas of interest in further depth," she said.

Molly called Jason back over the crackly radio, leaned back in her chair, and folded her arms. "What's going on? You never do that."

She sighed but was relieved she'd asked. It was good to have a legitimate reason for the weird stuff that was going on. "Matt wants to know if there is plane wreckage here. If there is, it's his job to figure out if there are any human remains that can be repatriated. I just thought we could give him a head start. Also, if there's nothing here, he can head back home." At least that had been the idea this morning, but every time she saw him, she wanted to drag her feet and keep him in Iraq with her.

"Fair enough," Molly said, looking solemn.

Jason, who seemed to be on his best behavior since this morning, was doing a great, detailed job sending electromagnetic pulses into the sandy earth. He refused to stop for water, and in the end, Harry made Molly take some out to him.

When lunch arrived with one of the cooks from the hotel, everyone stopped and sat under the awning that popped out from the trailer. It wasn't an awesome lunch by any means, certainly not to Ain's standards, but it was welcome by the time the midday sun had come around. Cans of tuna fish, crackers, and rice. In the heat, not too many people were hungry, but they all took the opportunity to get out of the sun and sit awhile.

From experience, Harry had known to bring large plastic ziplock bags for the local workers, and most of them put the extra rice and cans of tuna into the bags to take home to their families. As the chatter and eating died down, people started to wander back to work. Some site managers ruled the workday with an iron fist, but that wasn't Harry's style. She preferred having happy workers, and feeling confident when she left a country that she had done a little to improve the lives of the people living there.

She kept a close eye on Matt. After his admission that he mistrusts everyone, she was interested to see how he mitigated that. But she saw no evidence of suspicion, or unease, other than normal. So strange how people could hide what they were feeling. She wondered if it somehow destroyed their souls, keeping negative thoughts and feelings inside.

"Look. What do you think that is?" Molly asked over her shoulder from her position sitting on a cooler and peering at the small computer. "I'm getting some weird static here. I'm going to start the program, okay?"

"Sure." Harry hustled to her side and looked. Before there were programs to decipher the lines of static that came from the ground-penetrating radar, archaeologists had to figure out what the images meant themselves. Harry was old-school.

The image flickered across the screen like a radar image they show in movies. Then the composite pieces could be put together to make...

"What *is* that?" Molly said, craning her head to the side, as if that would help figure out what they were looking at.

Harry could see what it was. It was a perfectly rectangular void about the size of a sofa. The void meant that the GPR had picked up an area where there wasn't any sandy soil. It had to be something man-made, because of the perfect angles on it. But it could be a vault, or tomb, or a brick structure. It certainly didn't seem like wreckage, which she presumed would be random-shaped structures strewn about.

Matt was at her shoulder looking at the tiny screen. "What could that be?" he asked, and she repeated the thoughts she'd had.

"Man-made, you say." He stood up and looked out to the site.

"Yes, but I don't think it's part of a plane. At least not wreckage." She wondered if that made him feel better.

"Can you estimate its size?" he asked, digging in his backpack for something.

"Roughly. I'd say ten feet by, maybe, five or six feet, and I can't really tell the depth of it because the further down in the soil you get, the less accurate the measurements become."

He nodded and walked to the other side of the trailer. She heard him say, "Commander Jenks please," before he passed out of earshot.

* * *

"Sergeant?" the commander said. "Thank God."

Matt's adrenaline went into overdrive. He could feel the flash as it hit his heart and stomach. Fight or flight. He clenched a fist. "What is it, sir?" He almost laughed at how calm his voice was.

"I've got the classified file from a…old acquaintance in the Pentagon. Are you on a secure phone?"

"I'm using the satellite phone that I got when I arrived, so probably not." Satellite phones were notoriously easy to hack.

"Did you find anything there?"

"It seems so," Matt replied evenly.

"I thought so. People are already talking about it."

"Only the team here knows." Matt frowned trying to think if anyone had reason to talk about the find. "No one else knows. No one should have been able to get information on the find back to the U.S."

"Then someone there is not…friendly to your mission," his commander said carefully.

"Copy that, sir." *Cluster. Fuck.*

There was a pause at the other end. "Okay. Everything's fine. This is easy. It's on a par with Columbia. Your mission is to recover two pilots and a tech sergeant. I'll e-mail you the details to your personal account."

"Copy that, sir. I'll look for the e-mail." He pressed the disconnect button and turned slowly to look at the people working the site. Who was the enemy?

Columbia was the most dangerous mission he'd been on while in JPAC. His team had roped down from a helo on a mountain, and then had to rock climb to another point to try to recover a pilot from a transport plane that had gone down in the '60s but only recently been found. Unfortunately the drug lords hadn't got the memo and had assumed Matt's team was coming for them. The team, which included a former pararescuer, an archaeologist, and a special forces guy, fought off around fifty guerillas for two days before help came. With, thank God, no casualties except sunstroke and insect bites.

So he guessed he knew what to expect now. Shit.

He had to let Harry know. Give her the opportunity to get out of here before the shit hit the fan. He mentally accounted for all the firepower. The .22 on his waist, the gun that Mueen always seemed to have on him, although God knows whose side he was on. He called for Harry, and then beckoned her over when she looked up. No sense having this conversation with everyone else around.

"What's up?" she said.

"Can I access my Gmail account on your Blackberry?" he asked, stowing the sat phone again.

"I guess." She handed it over. "If you can figure it out, you can do what you want with it. All my e-mails just seem to be impatient ones from the foundation. They're badgering me for a report I haven't put together yet. So feel free to delete mine if you need to." She rolled her eyes adorably.

"What's your password?" he said, looking at the screen.

She didn't say anything, so he looked up. She had a pained look on her face. Oh.

He typed in DANNY, and the screen sprung to life. The twist he felt in his stomach was just the thought of another Columbia mission, nothing else.

Eventually he got his e-mail loaded. Commander Jenks had sent the e-mail from his own private e-mail, too. This didn't bode well.

The e-mail consisted of just four links and no commentary. The first link went to a Wikipedia page about the $6 billion in cash lost during the Iraq war. The next went to a *Washington Post* article from 2011, explaining that a lot of the cash had been found, but not all of it. The third and fourth links went to the obituaries of three servicemen: two officers, Lieutenant Colonel Grant Mathers and Captain Doug Carpelli; and one enlisted man, Technical Sergeant Mike Ranger; all killed in action, allegedly in separate enemy attacks.

So basically, this crew was on a black ops mission, maybe with the lost cash, which amounted to somewhere between $55 and $100 million—give or take Wikipedia's accuracy. Frankly he had no wish to stand in front of anyone who wanted that money. People kill for a fraction of that every day.

"What is it?" Harry asked. "You look concerned."

He wanted to laugh. He'd be "concerned" about a water leak in his house. "Concerned" if he accidentally missed a meeting. "Concerned" didn't exactly cover it.

He handed the phone back to her and told her to read the links. She sat on an upturned bucket and scrolled through the information.

When she looked up at him, she was pale, and her chin

trembled a tiny bit. He wanted to wrap his arms around her and whisk her away from all this. Take her to his house in Hawaii and let her wander the beaches in safety. He owed it to Danny to keep her safe. Owed it to him for what he'd already done. He would pay that debt, or die trying.

Chapter 13

Does this mean what I think it means? I mean…reading between the lines." She cursed herself for the slight tremor she detected in her own voice.

He got to his knees in front of her and put his hands around hers, which were still clinging on to the phone. "I will keep you safe. Depend on it." The warmth of his hands warded off the chill she felt even though it was sweltering out there. "People are coming. It's time for you and Molly and Jason to go home. You don't want to be standing between someone and that much money if you can help it."

No way. No way in hell. "I'm not leaving. I'm not letting anyone take that money from the Iraqi people. It's theirs. Also, if we go, who will tell Malcolm Rapson and his team? Do we leave them here and just hope that no one mistakes their site for ours? What about the people on the site to the north of us? I don't even know those people. Would you go warn them?"

"No," he said. "I'm sorry, but they're not my responsibility." He sat back on his heels, sliding his hands from hers.

"Matt. Listen to me. I'm not your responsibility, either. Those three poor men are your responsibility. We'll keep using the GPR to see if we can find anything that may be human remains. Although this technology isn't great for that, I confess." She was part-infuriated with him and part...nope, she wasn't going to touch that thought. Not now. Not when everything was going to hell in a handbasket.

He stood. "And what do you mean the money belongs to the Iraqi people? Last I checked the dollars were ours."

"Did you read to the end of the article? That money didn't belong to us. The U.S. froze all Iraqi bank accounts at the start of the war. They cashed them out and were delivering the money back to the Iraqi people to help rebuild after the war. Whatever happens, that money stays here," she said in her sternest voice. "I mean it."

"That decision's above my pay grade, sweetheart." The arrogant bastard was actually smiling at her. In a horrible, condescending way.

"And that's why I'm staying. I won't have you calmly obey orders to take the money back to the U.S. It stays here, and I can tell you this: that decision is not above my pay grade. You may have to fight me for it."

He actually rolled his eyes as he changed the subject. "You just need to make sure that Molly doesn't tell anyone the GPR found anything. Just keep going and make notes of where you find things."

"The program does that. I'll take charge of the laptop when we finish today." They walked around the trailer together to find the laptop unattended. Molly was nowhere to be seen.

Harry's heart sped up. "Where...?"

"She went to see the man, beyond the dune," a voice said from above them. Mueen.

Matt slowly looked up to the roof of the trailer and opened

his mouth to say something, but he stopped. Harry was glad he thought better of saying anything.

"Thank you," she said, her beats per minute reducing. Molly needed to be told to keep her mouth shut, although, unfortunately, it was probably already too late to stop her telling Jason. She was right. As she breeched the dune, both Jason and Molly were staring down at the sand as if they could see through it to whatever the void was.

Harry whistled through her fingers. Both their heads shot up. "You don't have X-ray vision. Let's keep going," she shouted. "Molly?" She waited as Molly left Jason and made her way to Harry's side.

"It's not much use if you disappear with the only other radio. We have to be more vigilant about each other's whereabouts, okay?" As soon as the words were out, she knew that she sounded angry. There was no hiding that from Molly. She tried to defuse the situation. "Did you tell Jason about the void?"

"Of course I did. That little rat was whining this morning about not finding anything; I just wanted to rub his nose in it a little."

Well, she couldn't blame her for that. Harry wanted to do the same thing. "I need to tell you something. But I don't know Jason well enough to share it with him yet. Will you promise to let me make that decision? No pillow talk or anything?"

"Pfft. He'll be lucky if he ever sees my pillow again."

Harry arched an eyebrow at her.

"Yeah, yeah, I know. He does have a sweet side. I think he's just too young to be comfortable working with and for women. And that makes him insecure and…well, weird."

Harry said nothing. She couldn't leave Jason not knowing that there was a possibility that he was in danger. But she didn't want to tell him anything she didn't feel she could trust him with, either. She pulled out Danny's wedding ring and rolled it between her fingers as she often did when she had problems. She looked down at the ring in the harsh sunlight. Maybe she *did* still live in the past. Maybe she was just compartmentalizing, thinking she was moving forward because she could have sex without thinking about him.

Of course this thought would occur to her when she had no time to think about it. Of course it would.

* * *

Of course that freaking security guard heard everything. It was his own damn fault. He'd forgotten that he watched from way up there like a gargoyle. And that look he'd given him, when he'd told Harry where Molly had gone. The biggest shit-eating grin was reflected in his eyes. Not his mouth, just his eyes. Matt clenched his fists around the anger at himself. He was better than this. Harry was such a damn distraction.

He found himself pacing as he thought. A quick glance upward affirmed that he was still being watched by the grinning bastard. He must have heard everything: the call to his commander, his discussion with Harry. Even down to her conviction that the money belonged to the Iraqi people.

Dammit.

"Can you come down?" he asked Mueen evenly. He hoped it was evenly.

Mueen looked for Molly and Harry who were already coming back toward the trailer, and nodded. He slipped down, to the roof of his van, and then jumped from there. He was a freaking ninja.

"I know you heard…well, everything. It's all just conjecture at the moment, but can I rely on you to say nothing for now, until I can get everyone to safety?"

Mueen looked at the ground, then back up at Matt. He seemed to be choosing his words carefully. "My only job is the protection of these people." He gestured to everyone on the site, locals and visitors alike. "I will do nothing to endanger them."

Not really good enough. "You understand what will happen if word gets out that there could be money here, right?"

"I understand perfectly what will happen if *our* money is found," he said.

Matt sighed. He'd cross that bridge when he came to it. "So I can rely on you…?"

"To help keep everyone safe? Yes." Mueen bowed to him, and he was sure he virtually clicked his heels. With an energy Matt couldn't imagine having in this heat, he vaulted back up to the top of the trailer. *Let's hope he is as good with a weapon as he is climbing stuff.*

Well, that little chat hadn't exactly inspired a lot of confidence. He sat on a sand-blasted lawn chair and watched everyone come and go. Some of the young kid workers gave him shy smiles as they passed him, carrying equipment around the site. He couldn't believe the heaviness of guilt that settled around him. Pressing his body inward to somewhere he didn't want to go. He felt guilty that he'd fought here, especially given that all the locals seemed so friendly, and even the damned security guy had opened his house to him. He was guilty that his focus had slipped from the dead troops to the money, and he was guilty, still, about Harry. In some respects, he felt he had defiled sacred ground.

Man, he needed a drink or ten. Maybe spilling his guts to

Nitro would be cathartic. No way was he going to drink more than a couple of beers, though. Last thing he needed was to be incapacitated when the shit hit the fan, as it invariably would.

Goddamn Harry and her stubbornness. Maybe he should talk to Molly about going home. Maybe she would be scared enough to persuade Harry to leave, too. It felt pretty manipulative, but all is fair in love and war—although he hoped this was neither of those things.

As the workday drew to a close with no mishaps, he relaxed a little, tension leaving the guilt all alone in his body. He puffed out his cheeks with relief as everyone got safely into their vehicles and started heading off.

Harry stuck the laptop into her backpack and stowed it in Mueen's truck. He was going to keep a close eye on that bag until Harry had time to see what else was under the sands of hell.

Everyone was unusually quiet on the way back to the hotel, even Jason, who in the short time Matt'd known him had shown himself to be a bit of a smart-ass, always ready with a quip or a mild put-down. Wonder what happened.

They pulled into the driveway just after the other group, led by Harry's date that night. Rapping? Rapson. Yeah that was it. He wondered if he should ask if they'd found anything, but he doubted they'd tell him. Maybe he could ask Harry to probe later. Matt was beginning to see that this whole thing was bigger than just Harry and her dig. He needed a plan, and he needed Nitro to help him with it. Even if he wasn't military anymore, David would lay down his life for Danny's wife. It was a code that you just didn't break.

Thank God he was here.

Chapter 14

Harry had seen Professor Rapson as soon as they got back to the hotel. They were unloading their truck, too.

"Still on for dinner, my dear?" he asked as she shifted her backpack across one shoulder.

"Wouldn't miss it!" she said, looking at her watch. "Twenty minutes? Down here?"

"I've been investigating a bit"—he tapped the side of his nose—"I think you'll be interested in what I've found out about the Megellin Foundation."

She stopped. Oh, shit. Did she want to hear it? "I hope you're not going to get us fired!" She smiled at the older man.

"No, no, no. Nothing like that. I'll see you in a little bit." He lifted his ancient-looking leather satchel and left toward the ground-floor rooms.

She hustled up the stairs and shivered a little as she unlocked the door. Knowing a bug was in the room made her feel like some unknown person was in the room with her. A ghost. Maybe, if she had the chance, she'd buy a cheap transistor in the market and set it up right next to the chair leg. But that probably still wouldn't ease the feeling that she was being...Her Blackberry rang. She looked at the caller ID. Dammit, it was the foundation.

"This is Henrietta Markowitz." She winced in anticipation of the response. She wasn't wrong.

"This is Mr. Randolph. You may remember that I'm the one who signs your expenses." Wince indeed.

"Of course, Mr. Randolph. How are you today?"

"Why haven't you filed your reports on your site findings?"

Ummm. "It's usual protocol to file a report at the end of the survey. We still have at least five workdays left."

"And yet I asked you for your initial findings yesterday."

Silence. *Make nice. He's paying everyone's wages.* "I apologize. I will get them to you tonight. May I ask what kind of things you're looking for? So I can put them up front in the report?"

"You may not. I'll expect your report before tomorrow, then," the abrupt voice continued. "An e-mail, Ms. Markowitz. I'll be waiting for it."

"Yessir." She saluted as she rolled her eyes.

He hung up.

"You absolute idiot. You don't know anything about archaeology. You want a fast and incomplete report? Well, I'll give you one." She hesitated, suddenly scared that maybe he hadn't hung up. But her phone definitely showed that she wasn't talking to anyone. Then she turned slowly to the desk chair. *Oh, shit.* She wasn't talking to anyone except the person listening in over the bug.

What the hell had happened to this easy, fast, lucrative job? She just wanted to get the hell out of here now. Too many pressures, too many uncertainties. This wasn't how she liked to live her life. She liked uncomplicated. She liked certainty. After Danny died she'd almost lost her ability to function, a normal symptom of grief, she now knew. But then it had seemed as if the world had stopped. The only way she managed to function was to take one step at a time, do one thing at a time. That's why she worked for herself.

She grabbed her notebook and started scribbling bullet points to include in the extremely interim report. Surface features. The sandstorm. She tapped the end of her pencil on the paper… the void, and the money, and the artifact. How much could she write? She'd have to try to figure that out with Matt at some stage that night.

Hmmm. She lay back on her bed for a second. Maybe after dinner she'd go to his room; maybe they could work on the report together, so it fit both their needs. *Their needs.* He was such a monumental jackass about the whole sex thing. She badly needed the mindless release of casual sex. *Urgh.* How many times could she say that to herself before it actually came true? Maybe she didn't need the release of sex. Maybe that wasn't why she wanted Matt. Maybe she wanted something different.

She put her notes in her black foundation file, got changed, and headed on down to meet Malcolm. Maybe they could compare contracts to see if they were actually doing the same work. She could also ask him if he'd been harassed for an early report.

He was waiting for her outside the restaurant, dressed pretty much as he'd been earlier except with a bow tie this time. God, she loved old English men. So proper. She smiled as he proffered his arm for her to take. She grinned as she slipped her hand around his arm.

Once they'd been seated, he took out a bunch of files from his briefcase.

"Wow. You seem to have much more information than I do." She waved her own thin file containing only her contract with the Megellin Foundation and various printouts and maps of the site.

"I'm an old, old man. I have nothing left to do except glean information." He smiled and winked. "No one takes me seriously because I'm so old. No one pays any attention to me."

Harry laughed. "You wily old man, you!" Suddenly she wanted to know everything he knew, to put him in her pocket and always have him around. "So tell me everything," she whispered.

He looked around them melodramatically. "Well, we're not alone, for starters."

"You mean in an *X-Files* way or…?"

"Megellin. They have more people here than just us."

Harry relaxed into her chair and took a sip of Diet Coke. "Well that's not entirely a surprise, since I saw you here. So where are the other teams working?"

"I don't know, but the lovely young lady who processed my visa said that they processed twenty-four visas together. All to come here. At least this town. Now, three were for you and your grad students, and four were for me and mine. That leaves seventeen unaccounted for."

Harry frowned trying to remember if she'd seen any other archaeologists around. "Well, there is some kind of excavation going to the north of our two sites, but I haven't seen anyone at this hotel. I just assumed they were staying in a town closer to their dig."

A waiter arrived to take their orders. There was very little meat available in Iraq outside of the huge cities, so she opted for a vegetarian lentil dish. Malcolm went for fish.

"I don't think that dig is a Megellin one. I don't know for sure, but I don't think so."

Harry shrugged. "So what other business is Megellin in?"

"And that, my dear, is the sixty-four-thousand-dollar question."

Harry laughed. "Why are you so interested in Megellin anyway? I just want to do the work and then leave as soon as I can. Have they been badgering you for a report?"

"Hmm? No. Why? Isn't it early for a survey report?" He peered over his glasses at her.

"Mr. Randolph was adamant that I submit an interim report tonight."

"How very strange. Have you found anything?" he asked.

Harry took a moment to take a bite of her lentil stew that had arrived. She valued his opinion, and she really wanted to talk to someone external to this whole mess.

"Kind of. Nothing old." She slumped a little, knowing she was going to tell him about the aircraft part, at least, and knowing that Matt would kill her later. This time she looked around. When her eyes met his again they were sparkling behind his glasses. "You're loving this, aren't you?"

"I'm an old man; this is as exciting as it gets."

"You're not that old," she protested.

"I know. But I get treated much better as an old doddery buffoon."

She shook her head. "Incorrigible. Anyway. We found a piece of military aircraft. The military thinks it might be a downed American plane from the war."

"Fascinating. Although…what do you think was on the plane?" he said, leaning forward.

What the...? "I have no idea," she choked, grabbing her soda.

"I mean, probably missiles right? Maybe guns? Other ammunition? I'm sure there are people who would like to get their hands on it. Maybe that's it?"

She hadn't thought about the weaponry that might have been on it. "I have no idea." She must remember to ask Matt what might have been aboard the plane other than the money. "Anyway, the military have asked me to keep it quiet, so I don't know what to put in my report. I mean, you know as well as anyone, if I'm caught being less than truthful on a report, I'll never find work again in this field."

"That is perfectly true. It sounds like both hands are being forced, and it's up to you which one you give in to. Your business or your patriotism." He gave her a sympathetic look.

"Ironically, I wouldn't have my business if it wasn't for the military." She took another sip and motioned to the waiter and asked for a glass of red wine.

"My husband was in the military. The air force. He died here in Iraq." She took a breath and met Malcolm's eyes.

"Oh, my dear." He patted her hand.

"It was the compensation they paid me that allowed me to go to school and set up my own business. That allowed me to come here."

"Don't be conflicted about that. That was them repaying a debt. Their debt. Not yours. You have to move past that. You don't owe them anything."

"You're English. I'm sure it's different there, but in the U.S., the military is everything. We do anything we can to help; we bend over backward for them." The image of her bent over for Matt in front of the mirror made her flush and take a hurried sip of soda. Jesus, he was never more than a rogue sentence away from her thoughts. She had to get that man out of her system.

"I'm sure you'll make the right decision for you. And if it helps, I'd hire you."

"You're very kind." She changed the subject. "So what did your phone calls reveal about Megellin?" she asked.

"That survey you said you did last year. Where did you say it was?"

"Kurdistan."

"That's right. Amersham College, right?" he said, shuffling through some papers in his folder.

"That's right." She remembered because Amersham was a town in the UK that she'd visited once.

"Doesn't exist. Not in the United Kingdom, Australia, Europe, Canada, or the United States. Or any English-speaking country that I've found. Do you find that odd?"

Impossible. Surely. "Of course I find that odd. I…I'll have to check my records when I get back to the room, see if I remember it right. I may have made a mistake." She didn't think so, though.

"You don't strike me as someone who makes mistakes like that. Don't get me wrong. Amersham College has a lovely website, with a very worthy mission statement. But no faculty, no campus, no tuition fee information. Nothing."

"That doesn't sound like a mistake; that sounds like subterfuge, doesn't it?" Hell, was her whole contract compromised? Who the hell was she working for? Instinctively, she looked around for Matt. She wanted to tell him what she'd found out.

"Anyway, I have someone digging into their financials, and she's very good at finding things like this. The money trail is the yellow brick road, she says. You've just got to follow it to find the wizard."

"Nice analogy." Harry smiled. "When will you hear? I'm suddenly a bit worried about who we're working for and what exactly we're doing here." It occurred to her suddenly that maybe the only reason they were here was to find something Megellin was after. She squeezed her eyes shut. Could that be true?

"I should hear anytime soon. Probably tonight, our time. I'll let you know first thing in the morning." He dug into his fish and rice, making appreciative noises, only looking up when the waiter came with their drinks.

"You don't sound too worried," Harry said, having lost her appetite quite quickly.

"Not much worries me these days, dear. I've got to the age where I relish adventures and intrigue. After all, I spent my formative years excavating muddy fields in the rain in England. All this is quite exotic to me."

She nodded and sipped her wine. She thought she was like that, but now she wasn't so sure. After Danny had died, she'd been maybe a little reckless, not caring too much one way or the other whether she was alive or dead. She took risks that others found unpalatable, and always embraced the adventure. But here and now, she was becoming scared. Not for her life, just scared that this situation was disorientating her status quo. Nothing felt like it would ever be the same again.

* * *

David Church was late, and it made Matt smile broadly. When they served together, he was always having to cover for his tardiness. He would run in late for briefings, uniform buttoned up all wrong, and a bed head making his short haircut look asymmetrical. Matt would shove the briefing notes into his hand and he'd pretend he'd been there all along. It gave Matt a degree of comfort that some things never changed.

He slowly drank his beer and waited at the bar, watching the people come and go, pinning notices on the board he'd clocked before, and smuggling alcohol up to their rooms. He checked the time and wondered how Harry's evening was going. Probably better than his.

He finished his beer and ordered some soup at the bar. While he waited, he went to read the posts on the bulletin board again. He didn't know why he was drawn to it. Maybe because of the sense of community it gave him. The feeling that people were visiting this country after the devastation of war and looking for travel companions to enjoy it with. It was as if normality had returned here. Someone came into the quiet lobby, and he watched as the man spoke to the man behind the small reception desk.

He looked back at the bulletin board, but just as he was reading about a weekend bus trip to Basra, the man walked back through the lobby toward the rooms. It was Mueen. Instinctively, Matt stepped forward toward the wall, to avoid being seen, and he wondered why he had. Maybe the security guard checked in with the hotel in the evening?

He checked that his soup hadn't arrived—it hadn't—and went out into the lobby. He looked in at the restaurant and saw Harry sitting alone. The whole place was virtually empty, so he wandered in casually. She did a double take when she saw him, but smiled nonetheless. Warmth rose in him. Her smile was one worth coming home to. *Shit, where had that come from?*

"Where's your date?" he asked as he surveyed the table. It was just empty glasses and papers. "Was it a working date?"

"Kind of. Malcolm just went to his room to fetch some papers that he'd forgotten to bring. I'm sure he'll be back soon." She looked at her watch. "He's been gone awhile, though." She sighed, and he pointed at a chair, asking silently if he could sit.

From beneath the table her foot pushed out the chair. "Sure. You will probably be very interested in the things that he's uncovered about the foundation that sent us here. But I'll let him tell you. I suspect he'll enjoy the audience." She smiled. "What are you doing this evening?"

"Waiting for David. We were supposed to grab a drink, but he's late." He laughed. "He was always late when we were in the unit. Always. Late for chow, late for meetings, late whenever we had to leave for anything. It was like he couldn't read a clock. He obviously hasn't changed at all."

"I didn't know him that well. He came around after the funeral with some of the other guys from the team." She paused. "You never came, though."

"I know. I'm sorry. I was a bit of a mess. I was there, you know. When it happened."

"Don't apologize about a thing. I don't remember half the people I saw, and I didn't know what to say to the visitors, anyway. I was a mess, too. And we were so young. No one that young should have to deal with that, and yet in that year so many of us did." She shook her head and smiled, pure life and vitality shining from her eyes. "Please don't blame yourself for anything. *Anything.*"

He had no idea what to say to her. So he just nodded slowly and looked for the waiter to order a drink. One came and he asked for another beer.

Harry checked her watch again. "He's been gone for twenty minutes. I feel as if my date was bored with me and has skipped out on paying the bill."

As if anyone would. He was about to say as much when the waiter came with his drink, but as soon as it was handed to him, someone shouted something in Arabic, and the waiter took the drink back from Matt's hand and disappeared with it into the kitchen.

He looked at Harry. "I didn't just…that really happened didn't it? My beer was here, and then it wasn't?" He had hoped to make her laugh, but instead she pushed up from the table and looked toward the kitchen, and then back to the lobby. He got up, too. "What's going on?"

"The police have been called. They're allowed to serve alcohol here, but they don't want to have any out when the police get here. Look." She pointed at the bar, which was being closed. Huge metal shutters came down from the ceiling around the actual bar, so people could still sit in the room, just not get any booze.

"Can you find out what happened? I can't be here if this turns out to be something hairy." His boss would kill him if he gave a statement to the police about anything, especially what he was doing here.

"Let me ask the man at the reception desk," she said, hugging herself around her middle. She was obviously getting the same vibes as he was: something bad had gone down.

He stood in the entranceway to the restaurant, watching her progress. She took a step back from the desk and turned toward Matt, one hand clasped at her chest, a look of pure anguish on her face. He stepped toward her, but she ran back to him, ushering him into the deserted restaurant again.

"He said the old Englishman was found dead in his room."

"Jesus. I'm so sorry, are you okay? Was it a heart attack or something?" He touched her arm. He wanted to hug her, but she was closed in on herself. Slightly bent over and arms wrapped around herself again.

"Not a heart attack. He said there was blood everywhere." She straightened. "Unless he had some kind of freak accident, he was killed, Matt."

Chapter 15

Just at that second, four policemen ran through the lobby with their guns drawn. Matt pulled Harry back. "Don't get in their way. By the way they were holding their weapons I'd have to assume that they're not highly trained."

Harry shivered and looked at the table she and Malcolm had been sitting at just minutes before. "These were all his research notes on the foundation we're working for..." Matt needed to know what Malcolm had discovered. "Listen, Malcolm had suspicions that we were sent here to find something specific, and given what we know..."

"Shit." Matt looked at all the paperwork. "Gather all this up, stow it in your bag, and just pretend it's yours. Don't let it out of your sight. Don't tell anyone you have it."

He was right. They needed to keep this. Maybe Malcolm had dug up the answers without really understanding what he had. She grabbed all the papers, shuffled them on the table so she could fit them all in the foundation folder, and slipped them back into the leather satchel that Malcolm had brought to dinner with him.

At that moment a low whistle came from the kitchen door. Both of them looked up. It was David.

"You should go with him. Get out of here, and come back when it's all clear," she said. No way did she want to get Matt tied up in hours, maybe days of red tape.

Matt beckoned David over. "You're a lifesaver. A fucking late lifesaver, but I'll take it. Someone has died in the hotel, probably murdered. A colleague of Harry's."

"I heard. We have someone monitoring the police frequencies, and they advised me because I had an asset here. Luckily I was already on my way." He grinned and snapped the gum he was chewing.

"I'm not your asset," Matt grumbled.

"I thought you'd prefer that to 'protectee,' brother."

"Fair point." Matt dug in his jeans pocket and pulled out his phone and gave it to her. Call us when the police have left. But don't leave it too late; I don't want you left alone. You stay downstairs, in sight of the police and the receptionist, until we come back, okay?"

She took the phone. "Sure." As soon as she said the word in an embarrassingly small voice both guys took a step toward her. Then they both glared at each other. "Get out of here, both of you. I can take care of myself."

"Press the pound key. It'll speed dial this"—David waved his identical phone—"and we'll come right back."

"Go," she said, lifting Malcolm's satchel onto her shoulder. She watched them pass through the door into the restaurant kitchen. Matt turned and cast one more glance in her direction before disappearing from sight.

She looked down at Malcolm's satchel and realized that she ought to stuff her small purse in there, too, lest it look weird that she had a shoulder bag and a purse just to come down to dinner. She sat in the not very comfortable chairs in the lobby and waited. Her heart ached for Malcolm, and whoever he'd left behind. She wondered if she should gather his team, but if memory served he had a deputy manager with him. Maybe she'd wait until the morning to see if she could help in making arrangements.

Taking a breath and closing her eyes, she tried to organize her thoughts and feelings. Malcolm had been killed. Malcolm had been looking into the Megellin Foundation. Malcolm had unexpectedly returned to his room when he was supposed to be having dinner. Maybe he interrupted someone looking for something? Her eyes dropped to his satchel. A shudder rattled through her so strongly that she looked to see if anyone in the lobby had noticed.

A few people had migrated to the lobby now, having been ejected from the bar. She should call Jason and Molly. She inched around the semicircular sofa until she reached the house phone. She called Molly's room and asked her to come meet her, and to bring Jason. Harry tried not to give a hint of what was wrong.

Molly came down the stairs first and waved when she saw Harry. As she was striding over to the sofa, she stopped when she saw a policeman talking to a hotel employee. Then came over looking askance at Harry.

"What happened? Are you all right?" Molly's brow creased. "You look awful. What happened?" she repeated.

"Malcolm Rapson died in his room. He went upstairs to get a piece of research, and he never returned."

"Oh my God, that's horrible. Are you okay?"

"I'm fine. Sad, but fine." In truth she was a lot more worried than sad. Something that she hoped time would reverse.

"Was it a heart attack? He always ate that British M&M-type candy. He popped them in his mouth all the time at that conference we went to. Remember? Smarties, he called them. Said he needed them to stay smart." Molly smiled at the memory and leaned back against the hard knobbly back of the sofa.

"I don't know what it was exactly"—she took a deep breath—"but the man at reception said that blood was all over his room."

Molly paled and braced herself on her knees. "He was killed? Who would kill such a nice old man?" She shook her head and then went still. "Do you get a weird feeling about everything that's happened here? The artifact you found, the constant e-mails and calls from the foundation…"

"You've been getting them, too?" Harry asked in amazement.

"Yeah, both me and Jason have. I've been ignoring them. Figured it was bad form for them to try to circumnavigate talking to you first."

"Do you think Jason has been talking to them?" She hoped with all her energy that he hadn't.

"I don't know, and I couldn't find him just now. So he must be out somewhere or avoiding us after this morning." Molly started tapping her hands on her knees as if she was impatient to go. She turned to Harry, still tapping. "None of this feels right to me. You?"

"Not much, no. Do you want to go home? I can arrange it, and it won't be a problem at all. I just don't feel like this is a safe place for you and Jason right now." It would be some kind of a blessing not to have to worry about them, but equally worrying to be alone. Except she had Matt, and David.

"Why don't you come home, too?" Molly asked, tacitly showing that she'd quickly made up her mind to leave.

"I can't. I can't abandon a job. We may never get hired again. They want a premature report, so I'll just give them one." Except if Malcolm was right, Harry and her team were not surveying for college students, but maybe for looters, or some kind of treasure seekers. She wasn't going to sit idle and watch something that belongs to the Iraqi people be taken, and if truth be told, she didn't trust Matt to do the right thing, either. She'd known enough military to know that they follow orders to the letter. If Matt was ordered to recover the money and take it back to the USA, he would. Unless she was around to exert some pressure.

"I'm staying. But it's absolutely fine if you need to go. There's more than enough work to keep you occupied until I get home, too."

"I'll think about it tonight," Molly said, frowning again. "Do you think we're safe in our rooms?"

"I'm sure you are if you lock it well." Then she remembered how easy Matt found it to get in. "Just make sure you use the dead bolt and jam a chair under the handle. I don't know if that works, but it's been in so many movies that I'd have to assume it might give you some security?" She shrugged and smiled. "I'm sure you'll be fine."

Molly stood up. "Are you coming?"

"No, I'm going to wait for Matt here. Besides, I don't know if anyone will tell the police I was having dinner with him before... I'd rather speak to them here than in my room." Although if the person monitoring the bug heard her talking to police, maybe they'd leave her alone.

Just as Molly was saying good night, shouting came from the corridor behind the staircase. Harry started, and clutched Malcolm's satchel closer to her side. Four policemen emerged, jostling and shouting at each other and those around them. Taking a closer look, they looked young and scared, and that seemed to be driving how loud their shouting was.

Harry grabbed Molly and pulled her down onto the sofa next to her. "Don't look at them," she ordered. Molly acquiesced immediately; she put her hands in her lap and cast her eyes down. Sometimes in Iraq it was by far the best thing to fade into the background, and luckily, being women, it was easier to be overlooked. She wished Mueen was here and wondered how to get ahold of him. He would know what to do.

Abruptly, boots appeared in her line of sight. She slowly looked up, knowing as soon as she saw the uniform pants that she was going to have to talk to the police. As she met his eyes, she smiled, hoping to pull off an innocent smile. Dammit. She *was* innocent.

A small man poked out from behind the reception desk. "Sorry, Mrs. He asked of me who Mr. was with before he…" His voice faded before he said the final word.

The policeman, who still had his gun in his hand, looked angry. Very angry. He motioned with his gun for her to get up, but he didn't step backward, so when she stood her face was inches away from his eyes.

* * *

"Where are we going?" Matt asked as soon as Nitro pulled out of the tiny parking lot of the hotel.

"We'll hole up at the Majestic. It's a fancier hotel a mile or so away. We'll wait for news. I have people at the hotel if we need help, Harry has your phone, the old man is already, unfortunately, dead. We're in a holding pattern until we hear otherwise."

He glanced at Matt, then back at the road. "They have a reasonable bar there, so there's that."

Matt nodded. He could do with a drink. But most of all he wanted Harry safely in sight, and Rapson's research into the Megellin Foundation in his hands. He should probably tell Nitro, but it felt as if he'd gotten his act together here, and he didn't want to cause him any trouble, or get him into trouble.

"Damn. I feel like I'm in a book, you know? The famous archaeologist is murdered, and no one knows why." He shook his head as he looked out into the dark of the desert.

"Except, in a novel, everyone else would start turning up murdered, too. Let's not tempt fate here. Let's just have a quick drink and see how the cards fall."

"My worry is that it's going to be much easier to blame a death on a foreigner. And that hotel has a lot of Americans in it."

"And don't tell me you feel responsible for them all?" David laughed. "Dude. You're not even here for them. You're here for three dead servicemen. Don't get all caught up in something unrelated. I get the whole Harry thing. That's different." His voice dropped. "That's Danny. But don't get confused about this. You are here to try to retrieve three sets of remains that may, although probably may not, be here."

Shit, he was right. He had to keep his brain on the job and out of the peripheral issues. He was trained for this. Trained to compartmentalize. But somehow everything had gotten tied up in his brain. The dead professor, Harry, Danny, the dead crew, the money, Harry, Harry…Suddenly he was really anxious to get back.

The SUV stopped and David hopped out in front of a huge Western-style hotel. Could have been in any city of the world. At least it looked anonymous. He climbed out slowly. Every fiber of his being wanted to be back at their hotel.

"Come on, brother. I've got your six. And Harry's. I'm not going to let anything happen. My company has huge resources that are in-play right now. If you go back right now, you're going to get involved in a police investigation that we can't control. Relax for an hour until we get news."

He was right. Matt shook off the instinct to go back and followed David through the lobby to the bar. It was exactly like every Hilton he'd ever been to. It was strangely comforting.

They ordered and sat at a small table against a wall. Matt couldn't help but laugh as they both made an attempt to sit facing the door, with their backs to the wall. Matt gave the high ground to David.

"So tell me about Harry. Did you know she was going to be here?" David asked.

"You could have knocked me down with a Crazy Ivan," he replied, referencing the paper targets they used to shoot at in training. "Worse thing is, I'd met her a few months ago at a party and never knew that she was Danny's wife."

David's eyes widened. "Oh man, tell me you didn't accidentally nail her. I knew your dicking around days would come back to bite you."

"Not exactly, but you know, close." He shut his eyes, trying to ignore how his heart had sped up. He didn't think it was guilt at sleeping with her now. It seemed to be guilt that he wasn't repulsed at the thought of it. He was guilty that he didn't feel guiltier? *Aw, fuck.*

Silence descended between them. David swirled vodka around his glass. "Did you ever, you know, speak to someone about what happened that day?"

Matt hesitated, then decided to be honest. "Nah. I thought about it, but I couldn't bear the thought of talking about it, you know. I just wanted to forget." And he hadn't. Not for one day.

"Do noises still bother you?"

Matt looked at him and frowned. How had he…But yeah, they had hung out together for a while after Danny's death. That's when he'd started picking up women. "Yeah, I guess. Not bangs, explosions. Just loud ambient noise, you know?" Except that was barely true anymore. It used to be that crowds made him irrationally frantic inside, but since he arrived in-country, a whole raft of other things was making him lose his iron-tight control. Iraq plus Harry obviously equaled bat-shit crazy.

"Same for me, for a while. The guy I…went to see, said it was the roar of the explosion and its aftermath that would stick in my head. You should talk to someone. It's been too long for you to feel this way."

He'd come to the same conclusion a day before. "Yeah, we'll see after this trip." He knew that the military was much more open about mental health these days. Seven years before, it had been a different matter. You'd say you were seeing a shrink in the same way you'd say you were seeing a friend's wife. You didn't.

He sipped his beer. He didn't dare have anything stronger.

David went on. "Do you see anyone else from the unit?"

"God…no, not really. You're the first I've seen in, like, five years I think. You know how the military is. They dispersed us around the bases. You?"

"Not since I punched out. War turns us. Makes us all different. Don't you think?" He raised his hand to order another drink, asking Matt if he wanted one, too, with the rise of an eyebrow.

Matt shook his head. Guess he'd be driving back.

When the waiter had left, he said, "What do you mean, 'makes us different'?"

"All my friends reacted differently to war. But I think we don't react to war, it exposes who we are, deep inside."

Hell, things had gotten serious, fast. "What did it expose in you?" Matt asked, somewhat dreading the response.

A flicker of dread passed across David's face for a second. Then he smiled, it not quite reaching his eyes. "My awesomeness, of course."

Matt didn't believe him in the slightest but was relieved that David had decided not to go the "heavy talk" road.

"Ah well, of course it did," Matt said. "For me it was my super-power of separating a woman and her panties within ten minutes of meeting her." He sat back in his chair with a grin.

They clinked glasses. Before they had a chance to drink, David's phone rang. Matt resisted the urge to grab it, and let David take it. He answered it and gave a slight shake to his head, indicating that it wasn't Harry. *Dammit.*

Matt checked his watch for about the hundredth time since they slipped out through the hotel kitchen. Just under an hour had passed. He took a breath and looked around at the other patrons of the bar. He'd clocked most of them as they'd walked in. Assessing people in public places had been ingrained in them from the first day of EOD training. That was back in the day when people actually stuck around to detonate bombs. Before suicide bombers had become de rigueur.

David hung up and filled him in. "According to the guys I have outside the hotel, the body has been removed, but the police are still there. They haven't called for reinforcements, so they can't really think the killer is still in the hotel. So that's good. We'll give it a bit longer, and I'll call my guy inside. Okay?"

"Sure. Not much choice."

"In a place like this there isn't much crime. This is probably the story they'll be dining out on for the rest of their police career. Don't worry. Besides, I have an in. My company trains and arms them."

Chapter 16

Harry's brain was going a million miles an hour. *Protect Molly, protect Malcolm's research.* She stood face-to-face with the policeman, who obviously didn't want to take a step back. With her heart beating so loud she was sure he'd be able to hear it, she slowly and carefully pushed Malcolm's bag toward Molly behind her back. The policeman's rudeness at trying to intimidate her resulted in him not being able to see anything except her pores, up close and personal. She resisted the urge to push him away.

Just as Molly had the bag in her possession, the young policeman grabbed her arm and walked to the middle of the foyer, pulling her with him. His grip was going to leave bruises. He wasn't local, she knew that much. She'd never been shown anything other than respect and friendliness from the locals. Still, she wasn't scared. She just wished Matt was here. Wished he could help, or that she could just be able to say good-bye to him.

Harry managed to gently toss the sat phone back at Molly. As the policeman started walking, dragging her in his wake, she said to Molly, "Remember to *pound* on that airman when you see him, right?"

"Right," Molly whispered.

Still holding her arm, he shouted at the other policemen. He was gesturing toward her and spitting out words that she had no idea how to translate with her rusty Arabic. Certainly this didn't look good. She wondered if she'd get more sympathetic treatment if she cried.

Suddenly a new voice came from behind them. Quieter, more reasoned. She couldn't turn around to see, but she swore it was Mueen. And then she heard as the voice invoked the name of the sheik who had allowed her to work there, and who supplied their workers.

Suddenly everything changed fast. She was released, and the man who had been holding her stormed off, out the front door of the hotel. She turned. It was Mueen. She wanted to hug him, but as American as he seemed, she knew it would be entirely inappropriate. Molly ran to her and wrapped her arms around her. "Oh my God. I thought I'd never see you again."

"Well, I was scared for *you*," Harry said, and she realized right then that she had to send them home. She wasn't allowing either Jason or Molly to decide for themselves. "Pack up your things, and we are getting you guys out of here. No argument."

"You're not coming with us?" she replied, as they stood watching the police peel out of the lobby in pairs.

"No. I am going to finish the job, send that damned report, and if I can't help Matt find the aircraft and whatever's in it, then I'll be on the next flight home. Promise."

Molly nodded. "I hate leaving a project undone, but I won't lie, this isn't like the last time we were in Iraq. It's like everything's shifted in a bad way. Not the countryside, or Mueen and Ain, or the people, just this place. I've just been getting bad vibes since we started at the site, you know?"

Harry smiled. "Are you sure it's not Jason giving you the bad vibes?" She paused as she remembered. "We still don't know where he is, do we. He wasn't in his room?"

"No, I knocked, and called his room on the landline. Nothing. He could have gone out?"

It was unlikely. The rest of the town was a few miles from their hotel, and to her knowledge he didn't have any transportation. He could have got a taxi or a ride from another hotel guest, she figured. "Okay, let's go to our rooms, and we'll poke a note under his door. I'll arrange your flights in the morning."

"Here." Molly shoved the satchel and the phone back at her. "You didn't really want me to hit Matt, did you?"

"What?"

"You told me to pound on Matt."

"No! Press the pound key for Matt. Jeez, Molly. You'd be a hopeless spy."

She grinned. "Good thing I'm an archaeologist then. Night!"

"Lock your door," Harry said and watched as Molly threw her a salute.

She gathered her things and turned to Mueen. "Thank you," she said simply.

"You're welcome. His Highness does not want any trouble for you. He also does not believe you would have killed your colleague."

"I didn't." She sighed as the real impact of Malcolm not being around hit her. A heaviness pulled at her lungs, making it hard to breathe. Unexpected tears sprung to her eyes. She reached up a hand and looked at the wetness on her fingers. She hadn't cried since…

Mueen stepped forward, but as if he had checked himself, he stopped abruptly. This evening was a train wreck. Malcolm was dead, and everything was weird. Molly'd been right. Iraq felt strange this time. "Thank you so much, Mueen. You saved us."

He bowed to her, silently. It made more tears prickle her eyelids. "Good night."

"Good night, ma'am," he replied, sounding as American as apple pie.

* * *

"All right. Enough is enough. I'm going back."

"Hmmm?" David said, presumably so he wouldn't slur.

"Dude. You've had enough. Let's get you a room here, and I'm taking your eyesore of a vehicle back to the hotel." Matt was pissed. No one was going to have his back if his backup was halfway comatose with alcohol.

"S'all right. I've got a room. S'where I live," David mumbled.

That pissed Matt off even more. He wondered if David ever intended on taking Matt back to the other hotel. Dammit. Well, too bad, so sad. He picked up the keys to the Suburban, and then took the sat phone from David's jacket pocket and propped him up a little better against the wall.

He handed the bartender some Iraqi dinars and asked him to make sure David got back to his room. The man nodded and sighed. This probably wasn't the first time David had gotten drunk here. Jesus. One more thing to worry about.

He left the hotel and got in the Suburban, shifting the seat back to accommodate his larger frame. He surveyed the car's interior. The extra handgun was still Velcroed under the dash, and there were all kinds of widgets and gadgets Matt had no idea how to use. He put his foot down and took off down the bumpy road. Except, where the hell was he? He'd been so concerned about Harry when they'd left the hotel, he didn't pay attention to where they'd been going.

He pulled over and found the car's GPS. Harry's site was listed, as was their hotel, David's hotel, MGL's office in Baghdad. So was an address in Mueen's village, which he supposed could be Mueen and Ain's address. That was weird. He got directions to the hotel and set off.

When he reached the hotel, it was in total darkness. No lights showed at the windows, no lights from the lobby. It was as if someone had pulled the plug on the whole building. The houses on the other side of the road didn't seem to be affected, though. Unexplained power outages were never good.

He took David's handgun and checked the rounds. Two missing. Four should be enough to accomplish what he needed. He locked the car by hand, not by the key fob, because he couldn't remember if the Suburban bleeped or its lights flashed when it was locked and unlocked. He stuck the gun in his jeans waistband, and he pulled out his shirt to cover it.

The lobby was quiet. No sounds from the bar, restaurant, or the reception desk. He stood silently in the middle of the lobby, waiting for some noise, or motion. Nothing.

Having grabbed a pillow from the world's most uncomfortable sofa to use as a silencer, he slowly crept up the stairs. He kept to the parts of the staircase nearest the wall, less likely to creak. Shit. He should have searched the car for night vision goggles. He was so out of practice.

As he reached the hallway leading to Harry's room, he stopped to listen. There were no sounds coming from any of the rooms. It was eerie. He took out his gun. His heart pounded in his ears as he felt his way along the dark corridor. He felt for the numbers on each door, until he found Harry's.

He knocked softly and got no response. Plan B: the credit card.

The door swung open, but it was light inside. Harry was standing directly in front of the door, toweling off her wet hair. His heart rate normalized and the fist that had been pressing against his stomach faded.

"What? You're breaking in for a slumber party?" Harry said, eyeing the cushion he was holding.

"That depends. You up for a pillow fight?" His shoulders relaxed, and he dropped the cushion. Her eyes widened at the sight of the handgun.

"Aren't there better ways to hide a gun than holding soft furnishings in front of it?"

"I brought it in case I needed a silencer." That stopped her in her tracks. He closed the door behind him and locked it. "Why the hell didn't you call? I've been going out of my mind with worry," he demanded.

She showed him his sat phone. "I tried, but it kept going to David's voice mail."

He dug the phone from his pocket. It was dead. He pushed the 1 button, and it powered up immediately. It wasn't dead. It had switched itself off. His jaw clenched and his shoulders started bunching again.

"How do you have light in here?" he asked.

She brought a lantern out of the bathroom. "It's solar-powered with a backup battery. Unfortunately archaeologists can't rely on there being a handy outlet wherever we need to work. I gave one to Molly, too. But just so you know, we haven't found Jason. He's been missing since before dinner."

"What?"

"Yeah. There isn't much we can do. Neither Molly's nor Jason's cell phones work here, so it's possible he went into town for dinner or something, but we won't know until morning, I guess. And, for obvious reasons, I can't go to the police. They nearly arrested me earlier."

A cold stream of dread ran down his back. Police prisons in Iraq were brutal. He couldn't imagine her in one. "Why didn't they?"

"Mueen invoked the name of the sheik. I don't know if it will hold them off forever, but I've got a reprieve, at least." She sat on her bed, running a comb through her hair that almost appeared translucent in the artificial light.

He sat at the desk and rubbed his hands over his face. It wasn't until he'd sat down that he remembered the bug. Aw, shit. He needed to be able to speak freely. Holding up his finger to her, he grabbed the bug and placed it on the edge of the basin in the bathroom. He switched on the extractor fan and closed the door. "You have to leave. It's not safe. Everything has gone to hell in a handbasket and I can't have you staying here in danger." As soon as the words were out, he knew he should have taken a moment to phrase that in a way that wouldn't make her—

"What? You can't tell me what to do! Will you get it out of your head that you're my protector? You're not. I didn't ask you to be, and it's not your job," she hissed, pacing the room.

He sighed, slid his back down the wall facing the door, and sat, gun cradled in his lap. He put the safety on. He said nothing. He was going to sit here until morning, until he knew that nothing unwelcome was going to come through that door. She was going to have to like it, or lump it.

She sat on the bed and watched him. "You're going to stay there all night?"

He nodded, stuffing the dropped cushion behind his back. He'd been in this very position a few times when he was still in combat. An ass patrol, they'd called it. Someone sitting guard over the sleeping team. He just never expected to have to do the same for Danny's wife. He never expected anything that had happened in the previous two days.

"Look, I won't deny things got hinky very fast here, but my ability to make a living hinges on completing the survey. Archaeology is a terribly incestuous field, and if anyone heard I hadn't reported, or didn't complete a survey, the words "looters," and "untrustworthy" would circle around my name, and I'd never, ever get work again. I need to do this. I need to finish this."

"How long will it take to salvage your reputation?" How fast he caved.

"I'm sending Molly and Jason home tomorrow, always assuming we find Jason." She worried a fingernail with her teeth as she paused.

"I'll find him. Tomorrow, though. Go on." He hoped he could.

"Then I think I could finish in one day. Maybe go home tomorrow night, or the following morning? Maybe. I hate doing a less-than-thorough job, but since Malcolm won't be able to file his report, either…maybe I can find his notes and complete his report, too. At least his staff will be paid, then."

"His research. Where is it?" Matt asked. "Didn't you say there was something you wanted to tell me?"

"Oh my God. Yes. I'm sorry," she said, jumping off the bed and grabbing Malcolm's worn old bag from her closet. "I mean, he said he'd done research on the Megellin Foundation, and… God, I can't remember what he said with all the…"

"Murder?" Matt said, trying to make her feel better.

"Give me a second." She closed her eyes and nodded to herself as if replaying the conversation in her head. It was adorable. *No, no it wasn't.*

"Okay, Malcolm said that the last survey I did for them wasn't subsequently excavated by students. Even though they told me that the Amersham College archaeology department was going to. He told me that the college didn't even exist. I couldn't figure out why they would do that, unless they wanted a survey for another reason."

"Like what?" Matt asked.

"Off the top of my head, maybe someone wanted to build there and wanted to be sure there wasn't any archaeological reason not to?" She paused, and he gave her a second to reach the conclusion he had. She didn't.

"Or they want to extract the artifacts or treasure without anyone knowing?"

Harry closed her eyes and sighed. "I can't imagine anyone doing that, but it's a possibility." She paused. "Malcolm thought the foundation wanted us here to find something specific. And I wonder now if they're looking for the same thing we are. In all honesty, I really don't know who they are. Just that they pay well, are well-known in the world of academia…and are unusually anxious to get our reports on this dig. And I suppose we can guess why."

"So your Megellin Foundation knows about the aircraft carrying the Iraqi cash. They know about it, and they sent your team to see what you could find. You found a piece of an aircraft, reported it, and somehow, that information got to them. That's all I can figure," he said.

"You think they are the ones behind Malcolm's death?" she asked, quietly.

She looked as vulnerable as she sounded. He got up slowly as if not to scare a stray animal, and sat next to her on the bed. "Let's look at his research together. See what we can find. It might not be that at all."

He took everything out of the bag and then peered inside to make sure it was truly empty. It seemed to be. As he laid the bag back on the floor, Harry was already leafing through pages, putting them in order and placing them in piles. He stepped away as she worked.

"I wish I'd checked Rapson's room for a bug. I wonder..."

Harry's head popped up from the documents. "Are you going to check? Won't the room be locked? It's a crime scene after all."

"I'm not sure the police here are that geared up to solve crimes. But there's only one way to find out. Lock the door behind me and don't answer for anyone but me. Even if you know them, don't answer the door, okay?"

"Sure. Do you need a flashlight?" she asked.

"You archaeologists seem better prepared than Boy Scouts." He laughed, taking it from her.

She tipped her head. "Better prepared than you, anyway."

He rolled his eyes at her and slipped out of the room.

Chapter 17

Harry jumped up and locked the door. For all her protestations, she hadn't wanted him to leave her. Damned if she was going to tell the overbearing man that, though. She shoved the desk chair under the door handle, although it was on a swivel base and, well, she knew it wouldn't keep the boogeyman away, whoever he was.

She was scared. She hadn't felt scared by anything in ages. But with Malcolm dying, and the airplane, money, and having Matt, Danny's friend, here seemed to confuse the synapses in her brain. Nothing was normal. Her even, regular life had erupted into a tsunami of uncertainty and unease. Harry wasn't even sure if she was equipped to deal with it anymore. After Danny, she closed down, deliberately creating a life that was hers and hers alone. Making sure she wasn't too close to anyone, making sure her life was smooth and untroubling. She figured she'd deserved the even keel of her life, after the nightmare in the aftermath of her husband's death.

She lay back on the bed, crinkling all of Malcolm's papers. In fact, she didn't want to read them. Didn't want to know what he'd found out. She worried that if she found one extra thing to complicate this situation, she'd implode. Breathing was good, though. In, out, in, out. She took deep breaths to calm herself. To try to put out of mind what was happening around her.

A knock at the door startled her. "It's Matt," he said.

She ran to the door and let him in, trying to find a normality in herself to show him, worried that her eyes would give away her fear. She turned back to the bed as he entered.

"The bug was there. I left it. No sense in disrupting the evidence, should anyone come to look. But you know what that means, right?"

She nodded, not wanting to say the words out loud. It was about the money.

"Did you find anything in Rapson's notes?" he asked, settling back on the bed.

"Not yet. Here, grab some and read." She thrust a sheaf of papers that she hadn't looked at yet.

She wanted to reach out and touch him, just to feel him. Solid. Present. But she continued reading, hoping she wouldn't find anything that would rock her carefully constructed world more than it already had been.

Malcolm's research was cryptic at best. Random notes and large passages circled with pen and annotated with nothing more than an exclamation mark or a question mark. All the Megellin papers had random letters underlined. Some kind of code? She put them all to one side. After about twenty minutes, she'd separated the academic notes from the "what the hell is going on" notes.

"Okay," she said putting a pile of papers on the floor. "Those are human resources and other administrative papers. What we have left are those that related to this survey, and his research into Megellin."

Matt picked up a marketing leaflet. "This is for MGL Security. David works for them. There's a big question mark on it. Was he going to hire them for extra security on the site? Do you do that kind of thing when you're overseas?"

"I guess, maybe? I've never had to, but if all this was happening without you here, maybe I would? I just don't know." More likely she would have ignored the problem and just carried on with her work. Head-in-the-sand-itis was what Molly called it.

Matt slid the leaflet into his pocket and picked up a different pile. "These seem to be trying to trace the ownership of Megellin. Who is the person who signed your contract?" he asked.

"Mr. Randolph. He's also been calling Molly and me nonstop, asking for an interim report, which I am supposed to provide him with tonight." She looked at her watch. Shit. She'd completely forgotten about that.

"Okay, let's make a list. We have missing money from approximately 2005. We have some U.S. military aircraft debris and hundred-dollar bills at the site. We have a foundation run by an unknown entity which seems hell-bent on finding what's here, and the added information that the foundation may be a cover for illegal excavations."

She tapped a pencil on her teeth. "Also Malcolm, and maybe a missing Jason. As well as a potential void under the surface of the site." As soon as the words were out of her mouth, the room phone rang with a hard, brittle clang. She grabbed for it. "Molly," she mouthed to Matt.

"Jason's back in the hotel. He was out with Katherine from Rapson's team, the little bastard. I've briefed him about the professor, and frankly, he looked more scared than anyone we saw tonight. He's packing and seems to be happy to be going home tomorrow," Molly said.

Her voice betrayed her words. She was upset that Jason was out with another woman. "I'm so sorry, Mol. If it's any consolation, you deserve better."

There was a little silence. "I never even saw a female on Rapson's team. Trust Jason to be able to home in on the only other woman on a dig."

"Are you okay?" Harry said.

"Sure. You live and learn, right?"

"I always have," she replied automatically, and then wondered what exactly she had learned since Danny died. To tuck her heart away from friends, colleagues, and lovers. To walk away. That's what she'd been doing for seven years: walking away.

They said good night to each other, and Harry hung up.

"Jason was catting around. He's back and packing, so we can scratch him off the list, thank God," she said. At that second the battery on the solar lamp flickered and died. For a second neither of them moved.

Harry knelt up on the bed and reached for the thin curtain. She yanked it back and let the slight light from the moon illuminate the room.

Matt got up and closed it again. "Let's not make ourselves targets. I'd rather we kept it dark in here than worry about passing the window."

"You think someone might shoot us?" A shiver trickled down her spine, making her grab a blanket and wrap it around herself.

"I have no idea, but we don't want to take the chance on the same night that Malcolm was killed, okay?"

"Okay? Not really. Not…" Her voice cracked. What was *wrong* with her?

In a second he was next to her, holding her, rubbing her back. "It's a lot to take, I know. I'm sorry your friend died, and I'm sorry this is happening to you."

"I don't know what's wrong with me," she said, trying to pull away from him and at the same time wanting to lose herself in the strength of his arms.

"There's nothing wrong with you. What are you talking about?"

She took a deep breath and scurried away from him, sitting with her arms wrapped around her knees and leaning against the headboard.

"The first time I came to Iraq, I wondered how it would be, you know. To visit the country where he'd died." She heard him shift on the bed. Was he uncomfortable? "If you don't want to hear this, it's okay. I'll stop." She had no idea really why she'd started talking in the first place, but there was this ball of…something…in her stomach that was full of unanswered questions and unrealized feelings. She just wanted to tell someone, in the dark, with no one looking at her, examining her face for unspoken feelings like so many had done since Danny had died.

"No, I'm interested." His low voice seemed to fill the room with a safe warmth. Dammit, girl. Get a grip.

"Our first time here was magical. It was spring in all senses of the word. Everyone was joyful the war was over and Saddam had gone. People who had been banned from praying for decades were able to pray openly for the first time. We met Mueen and Ain, who both seemed thrilled that visitors were coming back to their country. He traveled fifty miles each way every day to come protect us. That's why I was so happy to be offered a job virtually on his doorstep this time." She paused and sighed.

"I was so excited to come back, but from the minute we touched down, everything was different. The Iraqis seem more anxious than joyous. My own team feels discordant.

"The very first day, I found that piece of metal, and everything's been on a steep downward trajectory since then. You— no disrespect—and all the fun and games that you brought, the hundred-dollar bills, then Malcolm. It's like a perfect storm.

"My life is ordered, neat. And this is anything but that. Jason caused the first hiccup in the team by seemingly seducing and abandoning Molly. Then you came in with your surprising background and your subsequent recriminations…"

"I'm sorry about that. Really."

"Then Malcolm and his suspicions about my work. My work. The one thing that's kept me sane during all these years…I just don't know what to think. It's like the world is suddenly conspiring against me."

There was a pause, and she swore there was stifled laughter. "That's right. Everything that's happened, everything that's gone wrong here, it's aaall about you."

* * *

Matt heard her sharp intake of breath and wondered if he'd misjudged his attempt at lightening her mood.

There was a second in which he opened his mouth to explain, when there was a shifting in the air around him, and just as his lightning instinct had him reaching for his weapon, a soft projectile thwomped into his face, knocking him backward and off the bed.

"No one makes fun of my pain without incurring the wrath of the pillow ninja," she hissed.

Relief and outrage vied for pole position as he immediately planned his revenge. He let out an agonized groan.

"Oh my God." He heard her scrambling over the bed to the foot where he'd fallen from. "I'm so sorry, did you hurt—"

He reared up, wrapping his arms around her legs, and launched her back onto the bed. She bounced like a rag doll as he grabbed the cushion he'd taken from the lobby and swiped at her as she tried to right herself.

"Ooff," was the only thing she managed to say.

Victory is mine. "Truce?" he asked from a safe distance.

"My hand is caught in the headboard." She giggled. "I swear it's not a trap. I'm an honorable foe, unlike you. Look, or feel."

Still keeping his distance, he put out his hand where he thought her shoulder should be. It was soft. Heat rose in his body.

"Okay, airman, it's not my breast that's trapped, it's my hand," she said with a totally audible grin.

"Sorry." He thought he would run his hand up to her shoulder, then her arm to find her trapped hand, but it seemed all his appendages had minds of their own. He hesitated on her breast, feeling it swell beneath his palm. *Shit.* He stretched his hand out so just the center of it was touching her, and he circled it around her nipple. Its hardness tickled his palm. He meant to move it to her shoulder, but he swore he heard her groan. The sound sealed the deal.

His other hand found her flat stomach. He ran his fingers over her skin, making her shiver. "Does your hand hurt?"

"No," she whispered. It was a tacit yes to everything else.

He lowered his lips to her stomach and kissed her, feeling it undulate beneath his lips. Kneeling on the bed now, he ran his hands up and down from her waist to her legs, legs to waist, and then with the same motion, he hooked her shorts around his fingers and yanked them down. She gasped. He grinned in the dark.

"You're kind of at my mercy now, aren't you?" he said.

In an instant she wrapped her legs around his waist and tipped him over onto his side. Before he could recover, she rolled him over and sat astride him.

"I'm sorry? What did you say?" In the shadowy darkness she whipped off her tank. He could barely see her in the dark. No way. Nakedness or death? He grabbed her waist and held her as he sat up and pushed her down toward the foot of the bed. He used the few seconds he was upright to flick open one side of the curtain covering the small window. A faint blue light lit the room. Just enough to see her in.

"I guess you weren't really that trapped, then?"

"Not *that* trapped." She smiled up at him, and he was gone. He ripped his shirt off over his head and was about to undo his jeans when Harry beat him to it.

Her delicate fingers played with his fly, flickering touches on his hard dick through the denim. Grazing her nails along his length until he was desperate to feel her friction. As if she read his mind, she flattened her hand and pressed hard against him, making him groan and push himself against her. She undid his fly, and when the heat of her fingers touched his flesh he closed his eyes and allowed his whole body to feel her.

Enough. He wanted her, right now. Stripping off his jeans, and managing to extract a condom from his wallet without fumbling, he retook the bed. He slid his whole body across hers touching every part of her with every part of him. She fit him perfectly. In every way.

"Fuck me," she said in a gravelly voice. "Fuck me hard."

No. Not this time. But he wasn't going to argue the point. He slipped on the condom, worried he wouldn't have the discipline to do it in about three minutes' time. Matt was determined to make love to her. He had been harboring a strong suspicion that she was so open, and so forward to avoid a connection. To avoid feeling anything. And if he had to deal with his feelings, she was fucking going to have to deal with hers.

He knelt between her legs, moving her easily onto his lap. Stroking her clit oh so gently until her breathing became faster, he slid into her, almost exploding himself as her tight sheath hugged his dick so tightly. He rocked her slowly against him. She reached for his face, and angled her half-open mouth over his, as if waiting for permission. He took her mouth slowly, slipping his tongue between her lips, tasting the toothpaste she must have used before he arrived. Her hot tongue danced slow patterns around his mouth, sliding against his tongue with the same cadence as his dick inside her. Heat pulsed in time between them, his thumb lazily used her own wetness to run circles around her clit. It was as if everything was moving to the same beat. The same clock. The same detonation sequence. It felt like something more than fucking.

She dragged her mouth away from him as she grasped him to her, nails digging into his shoulder blades. She gasped sweet breaths of air as he felt her tipping slowly over the edge.

Her pussy pulsed around his dick, seemingly pulling him farther into her. He laid a little more pressure on her clit as she threw her head back, gasping his name. Heat tightened everything below his waist, his balls, the small of his back blazed in a flash of release as he came. She rocked against him, milking the last of his climax from him.

He held her tightly, her breasts pressed against his chest, her legs wrapped around his waist. His mind flashed on the restaurant in D.C. The look of anger and defiance when he'd reacted so badly the first time they'd had sex. Every conversation they'd had. The resolve in her eyes when she'd talked about how the money belonged to the Iraqis.

There was no way he was letting her go. No way in hell.

His.

Danny's.

Shit.

Chapter 18

So, our operating theory is that Megellin Foundation knew about the plane crash somehow. And after maybe ten other digs along its flight path, they eventually found some evidence of it at my site."

"Correct. At least for want of a better hypothesis." Matt said.

Halfway through the night, the power had come back, meaning all the lights and the radio came on in the room, waking them both. After ten minutes of trying to get back to sleep, they agreed to finish Malcolm's papers. It hadn't been a fun read. A zipped inside pocket of his satchel had produced a thumb drive with the reports from the last twelve surveys Megellin had commissioned. No commentary, but when Matt had plotted them on a map, ten of the sites had followed a straight line from the air base outside Kuwait City into Iraq. Harry's site was their eleventh attempt at finding something. And it was pretty clear that they had found it.

Despite the seriousness of their situation, Harry's attention wandered from the paper. Matt's brow was slightly furrowed as he sat on the bed and sorted through papers. Every part of her wanted to reach out to him. To touch him, stroke her fingers down his tattoos. Was that…something other than just sex? It had been so long that she felt…was it affection?

She looked back down and bit her lip. She couldn't feel anything for him. That wasn't part of her play. Dammit.

"Don't bite your lip. That's my job," Matt said, grinning. "Come here."

"No." She tried to cut him off at the pass by giving him a stern look, but it only served to make his smile broader.

"Come here," he repeated.

When she didn't immediately move, he lunged across the bed and dragged her over to him, dumping her unceremoniously on his lap. She slid her arm around his neck to keep her balance. It didn't seem fair that he was so much stronger and bigger than she was. He was really just so much more everything.

He kissed her mouth gently, chastely even. Just the feel of his lips soft against hers stirred an unfamiliar tension in her stomach. He wrapped his arms around her and nuzzled her hair and then continued to read. It was…intimate. In that second she wanted to stay there, on his lap, forever. Flashes of Matt in her house, her yard, puppies running around their feet.

She jumped up, making out that she needed to get some papers from the desk. She put both hands on the pockmarked wooden surface and took a breath. This. Was. Not. Happening. She was about to turn around and tell him that she couldn't do this… closeness…when her Blackberry rang. She grabbed it and looked at the ID. Because they were in Iraq, it showed just the phone number, but she recognized it as a Megellin number. She'd have to tell them about Malcolm. She picked up.

"This is Henrietta Markowitz," she said.

"You didn't file your report last night, so I'm releasing you from your contract. That also means your flights have been canceled and refunded. Are we clear, Ms. Markowitz?" His voice was cold.

Shock sent cold trickles from the top of her head to the base of her spine. She sank back down to the bed. "Mr. Randolph. Professor Malcolm Rapson was murdered last night. The whole hotel was under police control. I couldn't…"

"Well, that's very sad. But that doesn't mitigate your abject failure to produce the required output. Your contract has been canceled. Good day to you." He hung up.

"Shit." She looked up at Matt. "I've been fired. He didn't think that Malcolm being killed was a good enough reason for me to not file my report. He's canceled all our flights. I'll have to book new ones. Shit. I wonder if I need to book one for Jason. I wonder if I can even get ahold of him."

"I'm sorry, but at least that's one thing we don't have to worry about now."

She looked at him questioningly.

"Your survey. We don't have to worry about you finishing. My plan is for you to leave here, go back to the U.S., and let me and David handle the situation until the rest of my unit and some official security gets here," Matt said, folding up the map.

"No way. If I leave you to your own devices, that money will never get to where it should go. I want the people in this country to have a better future. This money can mean schools and wells and better housing. I want Danny to have died for something good." She swallowed. "And I don't like saying this, but I don't trust the government to do what's right instead of what looks good politically. I'm sorry, I just don't." Why was she being this ornery? She had no idea why she was trying so hard to piss him off. And it was working.

"I don't think you understand what's happening. I mean, could you be so obstinate that you really don't realize how much danger you'll be in? If my team and I don't end this now, people will probably be after you forever. Do you get that? Anyone close to you will be in danger, too. It's killing me to have to send you away, when I want to have you in sight 24/7 just so I can be sure you're okay. But having you here is not going to get the job done. It's going to inhibit me doing my job." He paced up and down the small room, as if the space wasn't big enough to house his frustration.

"Your job?" she asked, painfully aware that her voice was raising almost loud enough for the bug to hear her through the running water. "Your job being Grant, Mike, and Doug, right?"

"Who?" He stopped pacing.

"Exactly. *Exactly*. The men you are supposed to be finding? Remember them?"

Matt dropped into the chair and held his head in his hands. "Fuck."

"It's okay." Her fingers itched to reach out and touch him, but she was afraid to get close to him. Afraid of what that would mean. "I will do anything and everything to help you recover those men, but not the money."

He raised his head. "You…you being here is fucking with my head. You're inextricably linked to Danny in my memory, and it's messing with my focus. My need to keep you safe is…"

"That's what I'm saying. That's on you. You need to sort that out. I'm not going home because of something that's going on in your head. Clearly, we've both got…issues, but that doesn't stop us from doing what we have to do," she said, she thought fairly reasonably. "Look, I have to arrange Molly's and Jason's travel downstairs with reception. Why don't you figure out a plan that doesn't involve me going home, and we'll reconvene over breakfast."

He nodded, remaining silent. His eyes were blank, and she wondered for a second if she'd broken him. "All right?"

He nodded again. She sighed, puffing out an exasperated breath, and left him there, wallowing in his own…whatever he was wallowing in. Last night had been amazing, but an amazing she needed to tuck away somewhere safe. She was afraid that if she let her thoughts and feelings leak out, she'd never stuff them back in again. He was doing a number on her head, too. Her head. Her heart. The heart she'd locked up since Danny. She was not going to start having feelings for someone, here and now of all places and times. Not going to happen. She stomped down the stairs and tried to remember what kind of air tickets she'd gotten the team.

The lobby was chaotic. People with bags were trying to get the receptionist's attention, there was a line for the lobby phone, people were tripping over luggage, and everyone seemed to be shouting about something. She took it all in from the second-to-bottom step, until someone with a huge suitcase virtually pushed her down the other step, trying to get to the lobby.

"Sorry, love," he said in a Scottish accent.

"What's going on?" she asked, grabbing ahold of the handrail.

"The police want to interview everyone at the station. And that is bad news. Apparently few who go there return. Everyone's trying to make a break for the border. Me included. Excuse me." He turned away and melted into the crowd.

She climbed back up a few steps and scanned the crowd to see if she could see Molly or Jason. They weren't in the lobby, so she pushed her way through the noisy groups and looked in the restaurant. No one was in there except for a few waiters hovering by the buffet and talking anxiously together.

After negotiating the lobby again, she took the steps two-by-two back to her room. She flung the door open, planning to enlist Matt's help in finding them, only to find the door blocked by baggage. She could just about wriggle through the space left for the door. Jason was sitting on his expensive hard Samsonite suitcase, and Molly was sitting cross-legged on the bed. Matt was standing by the window eyeing the scene warily.

"Downstairs is chaos; apparently the police are due to arrive and no one wants to talk to them," Harry said as she squeezed through the bags strewn across the floor. "I don't remember either of you bringing this much," she complained.

"We did. We just never had it all in one room before," Molly said evenly. "So how are you springing us out of here?"

How indeed. "I think the best idea is to get Mueen to take you to the airport and see if he can pull some strings to get you booked on the first flight. There's no point waiting here for an outside line, or to check out downstairs. You just go, and I'll check you both out later."

"I'll go down and wait for Mueen, then. Tell him the change of plan," Matt said, seemingly eager to get out of the fast becoming claustrophobic room.

"Ask him if he'll meet us around back. Frankly, getting through the throng with all these bags will be a task in itself," Harry said.

"Besides which, I don't think it's a good idea that you should be seen, especially if the police are on their way."

Jason spoke for the first time. "Look, I'm not sure if I'm going to go. I may stay and help out, you know?"

Silence descended. Harry took in Molly's bowed head, as if she didn't want to catch anyone's eye.

"I'm sorry, Jason, I appreciate the sentiment, but you're

contracted to my company, so I need you to be on the plane. The insurance just to have you both here with me was astronomical. If something happened to you, and I had an opportunity to take you out of danger and didn't...well, suffice to say, you'd be getting my first-born child."

"I'll sign a waiver." His voice was flat, determined. Basically, as unlike Jason as she could remember hearing.

Molly's head snapped up. "I'm sure Katherine needs someone to look after her now that the professor isn't here anymore, right?"

"It's not personal," was all he replied.

"I can't force you to get on the plane, Jason, but I will need you to sign a waiver, and I won't be needing your services. I will of course pay you through to the end of the week when we were supposed to go home."

This was so weird, and unlike Jason. But what did she know about him, really?

"You write it, I'll sign it," he said, fiddling with his phone.

"Do you still need your room?"

"Nah, it's okay. I think I'll move to the Majestic. There's more going on downtown."

"Okay?" Harry said, glancing at Matt, who shrugged.

Jason jumped up, and put together his bags, and pulled out the handle of his hard suitcase. "It's been great working with you."

"Hold it." Harry lunged for her work folder and pulled out a bunch of confidentiality agreements that she kept handy in case they co-opted someone else to help them. She crossed out a few items and added a sentence or two. "Here, sign on the dotted line."

Jason read it quickly, and signed. "Seriously, I learned a lot. Thank you."

"Thank you for your help. Maybe we'll see you Stateside," Harry said as he opened the door.

"Sure," he said very unconvincingly and disappeared.

* * *

With Jason's departure, the estrogen level jumped in the room to uncomfortable levels. Harry had her arm around Molly, comforting her for some reason.

"Don't worry. I'll have David look out for him. He's at the Majestic, too. I'll go find Mueen and tell him to come around to the back of the hotel."

Harry just looked at him with a pained expression on her face. He didn't have time to figure out what was going on here. "Which reminds me: I need to check in with him. I left him a little drunk last night." He grabbed David's sat phone, his wallet, and the keys to the Suburban. "I'll give him a ride there. Listen. Do not leave the hotel. Send Molly down to Mueen, but don't go anywhere until I get back, okay?"

"Sure." She sounded distracted, and he wanted nothing more than to wrap her in his arms and soothe her furrowed brow away. But he didn't.

He went down to the lobby. Most of the people were migrating to the driveway, presumably waiting for taxis. He found Mueen waiting farther down the driveway, on the other side of the road from the hotel. "Can you take Molly to the airport? Harry's taking her to the back of the hotel, to avoid all this." He waved at the hundred-plus people pushing themselves and baggage through the tiny front doors.

Mueen just nodded and climbed back into the truck and started the engine. Matt watched him reverse and take a small service road toward the back of the hotel. Jason. Where the hell did he go? He pushed back into the hotel and looked around. No sign.

He wasn't outside, either. *Oh well, he's not our problem anymore.*

Matt took the Suburban back to the Majestic hotel and called up from the reception to David's room. There was no answer. He looked at his watch. He supposed it was feasible that he was already out and about at nine a.m. Maybe MGL Security had an unlimited supply of black obtrusive Suburbans. It wouldn't surprise him; the last time he'd been in the Green Zone in Baghdad the streets had been full of them.

He decided to hang around in the lobby until he found someone who looked like they could work for MGL Security, or until Jason or whatever his name was, turned up. At least then he could give Harry some peace of mind.

Ducking into the restaurant to have a quick look around, he found David in a booth, chowing down the breakfast that treats all hangovers. Except it didn't even seem as if he had one. He dropped down opposite him and grabbed some toast off his plate before David could even react.

"'Sup, bud?" David asked, pushing his toast plate toward Matt.

"'Sup yourself? Did you get to your room all right?" he asked mildly, even though he wanted to rip him a new one for ditching him.

"Yup. Always do." David sucked a bit of food from his tooth and grinned. "You got back to the hotel okay?"

"Yup, I always do," Matt mimicked, "especially when I get to drive your target car."

"Oh yeah, I wondered where my keys and phone were." He took a gulp of coffee.

"The phone was switched off," Matt said, still trying to keep an even tone.

"Awww, don't be mad. I just wanted some drinking time with my buddy."

Matt suddenly didn't believe him. Didn't believe Nitro had his back, didn't believe he wasn't involved somehow in Harry's situation. A fist of betrayal jabbed in his stomach. They were brothers...closer than blood brothers, and David being a part of what he was trying to protect Danny's wife from was... incomprehensible, and utterly comprehensible at the same time. David's need to drink, his "living the dream" life here with all the weapons and booze he could manage. Some ex-military loved the security contractor life. All the action of the military, none of the rules, and much, much more money. He'd thought more of David, but maybe he shouldn't have. It was an easy trap to fall into. He fought to keep his face impassive, didn't want to tip his hand. Keep your friends close...

"Well I'm keeping your car, dude. You forfeited it when you were the first to pass out." He tried to put a grin on his face, and he covered his less than stellar attempt by taking David's coffee cup and swigging from it.

"I already have another one being delivered this morning. No sweat."

Matt really wanted to get back to Harry, but he also needed time to figure out what David was doing. He raised his hand to the waiter and asked for eggs, toast, and coffee, making a point to have it put on David's bill.

David laughed. "I don't mind. We have deep pockets. What are you doing today?"

"Not much, just putting some archaeologists on the first aircraft out of here." He watched David's reaction.

It was a relieved one. "Good." He breathed a heavy sigh and put his fork down. "Good, man. It worried me having her here. That's good. That makes everything"—he stopped and shook his head—"Well, it's safer for her, right? Takes a load off."

Matt just nodded. David's complexion flushed a little, and it made Matt realize how pale he'd been before.

A woman approached the table. Around thirty maybe, long braided dark hair, and a very athletic build. She slid into the booth next to David. He continued to eat. "Matt, Maggie, Maggs, Matt."

Matt wiped his hands on his napkin and reached across the table to shake her hand. It was dry and strong. "You MGL, too?"

"Yup," she said waving down a waiter. "And you must be his unit buddy from EOD, right?" She was sizing him up as she spoke. She also had a heavy London, England, accent.

"British?" he asked.

She grinned at him. "Sometimes." Then she continued in a very convincing deep Southern accent, "And sometimes I'm really not British at all, y'all."

David laughed. "She's ex–British M.I.," he said. "A real catch for MGL, in my opinion."

Maggie didn't accept or deny the compliment; she just ignored it.

"Military Intelligence? Why did you decide to leave? I hear that's pretty much a lifelong career if you want it."

She looked at him and cocked her head. "The question is, why haven't you left yet? David tells me you were a crack combat troop, the best in your field. And now you're what? Digging up dead people?"

Fury flashed through him. He recognized a deflection when

he saw it, but he wasn't biting. "And you went private because… a mission gone wrong? Killed someone you weren't supposed to?"

Her mocking face closed up.

"Oh, I'm right. Was it a colleague? Better watch your back, David." Matt couldn't resist. Two could play at her game. He wondered what branch of Military Intelligence she had been in. How dangerous she could be.

"Don't piss her off, Matt. She's not as nice when she hates you."

"Don't worry, just dishing her own medicine back, seeing if she can take it." He grinned at her. "We're cool, right, Mags?" He deliberately used the familiar name David had used. Fuck. He had to get out of here. He was just meeting people and making enemies when he needed all the friends he could get.

She rolled her eyes at him.

"Okay, gotta go." He wiped his mouth with the napkin and stood up. "Doing anything fun today?"

David glanced quickly at Maggie, a look she didn't see, but Matt did. Was it a warning? "Just patrolling. Nothing fun. See ya later?"

"Sure. Thanks for breakfast. Maggie, it was nice meeting you." He held out a conciliatory hand, which she made as if to shake, but picked up her coffee cup instead. She looked at him blankly.

Okaaaaay.

Chapter 19

Mueen got back to the hotel before Matt, and rather than waiting around for the police to pounce on Harry, he suggested they go to the site, where at least they were closer to the sheik's residence in case anything happened. It was a good call. She stashed Rapson's satchel under her bed for safety, left a note for Matt telling him to meet her there, and jumped in the truck.

"Are you sure you don't want to go home with Molly? I have a concern that everything is going bad," he said.

She sighed. "Not you, too. I just want to finish the job, file the report, and…" And make sure the millions of dollars get to the right people. It didn't matter that she'd been fired; she needed to be able to say she filed a report in case a prospective client asked. Then it hit her. She remembered what Malcolm had surmised. The first thing he'd surmised. That it wasn't money on board, but a weapon, or a missile, or even a nuke. Maybe that's what this was about. A chill went through her. How could she have forgotten to mention that to Matt? She suddenly wished she'd waited for him at the hotel. Crap.

"Whatever you are not telling me, it isn't worth your life, I promise," he said in his lilting accent that had become so familiar to her.

She stayed silent. She didn't have a good answer for that. She was scared. She thought she was scared. She couldn't remember being scared of anything after Danny died. A heaviness in her stomach, making her appetite disappear, making her shoulders bunch up. It was either fear or constipation. The only time she didn't feel that way was when Matt's arms were around her.

"How's Ain?" she asked.

A lightness came over his expression. "Making a nest for the baby, I think. Everything in the house is being changed and cleaned. It's a mystery to me. But she seems happy."

"I think that's a normal hormonal reaction to being ready to have the baby," she said. At least, that's what she'd heard. No one she knew well had had a baby. She realized that her life wasn't really normal. Her closest friend was Sadie, who did something with the government that they never talked about, and there was Molly, but she hadn't been really close to anyone in years. No weddings, no baby showers. Was she even living a real life? Work and…what? Casual hookups that by design didn't mean anything? She shook her head. She would think about it when she was home. Alone.

They arrived at the site, and as they drew closer to the trailer, she viewed the dunes. Could there be three servicemen under the sand here? Sorrow descended as she thought about their parents, or maybe wives and children. She shivered even though the air was dry and hot.

"Miss Harry? Did you give anyone permission to dig here?"

She rummaged around in the backseat for her bag. "No, *I* don't even have permission to dig. Why?" She straightened to see two figures dressed head to toe in black in the distance. They were too far away to see any features or how big they were. Sand was a lousy place to try to identify anyone's height or weight. "Maybe they're just passing through? I mean we only planted flag stakes to mark out the site. Because we're not digging I didn't put up any KEEP OUT signs," she said.

He climbed up onto the trailer as he usually did. "I will keep my eyes on them."

"Thank you." Harry opened her laptop and loaded the geophys program she had been using the day before. With everything that had happened, it felt like a week before. But it was really just yesterday that Molly and Jason had found the void in the electromagnetic pictures.

She mapped the points more carefully on the laptop, then searched for the maps she'd roughly marked up the day before. They were usually tucked in the laptop case, but they weren't there. *Huh?*

How could they have disappeared? There was no way they could have fallen out, as they fit snug against the PC. She dropped onto the cooler and tried to piece together where they could have gone. The only time they could have been taken was while she was dining with Malcolm.

For a frightening second she wondered what would have happened if she'd gone to get something while the thief was in the room taking her maps. Might she have been killed, too? Her thoughts flitted to Molly. Thank God she was out of this.

She looked up at Mueen. He had some kind of scope that he held to his eye. "What do you see?"

"They are not Iraqi," he said simply.

"How can you tell?" She stood and peered into the distance.

"Only in American movies do desert people dress like that. *The Mummy* or *Sahara* maybe. Not here."

Harry stifled a laugh but failed to keep it totally in. She

giggled at the thought of Western people dressing up like they'd seen people do in the movies, but as her teeth clattered together, she worried her mirth was verging on the hysterical.

"Get into the trailer and stay there until I come to get you." Seems he was just about as much of a bossy-pants as Matt was. But she didn't argue.

A few minutes passed with Harry crouched under a window, gnawing her nails. A strange adrenaline flooded through her. Not the same adrenaline as when she had canoed the Amazon in the night, nor when she had traversed two peaks in the Alps, only a thin rope keeping her from plummeting to her death.

This adrenaline was tempered with something else. Something new. Something that made her insides itch with…she shook her head. It was just an alien feeling, but it made her want to run from whatever was happening here. And she'd never run from a rush before, never turned down a life-threatening stunt.

She eyed the large blue cooler that usually housed water and doubled as a stool. She could probably fit in there if she needed to hide. She may never straighten out properly again, but yeah, she could fit.

Mueen sneaked back into the trailer. "I'm taking you to His Highness. It's the only place I can protect you. Both those people are carrying guns and a map. They are looking for something that they will obviously shoot to get at."

A coldness coursed through her blood. She trusted Mueen; at least she thought she did. But he'd never mentioned taking her to the sheik before. Never suggested they go somewhere together, alone. She fought her conflicted thoughts into submission.

"No…no. We'll stay here and wait for Matt. At least then he'll know where to find us."

"We must go now. I insist. For all I know, one of those people out there is *Matt*." He spat out his name in a way she'd never heard this gentle-voiced man speak before. It terrified her.

Suddenly he barked some Arabic words into a radio she'd never seen before. She was virtually paralyzed with the turn of events. She wondered if she'd be safer with the men outside. Her fists clenched as she tried to judge how quickly she'd be able to get to the door.

The sound of a diesel engine outside made her jump up. "He's here. It's okay." Before Mueen could react, she'd flung the door open. It was like she'd triggered an explosion. Incredibly loud bangs came from the Suburban that had just pulled up. Was that David? She cringed and ducked as the trailer door swung closed behind her. *Crap.*

"For Christ's sake, get back in the trailer!" Matt shouted from the vehicle.

She shook her head. No way was she going back in there alone.

He flung the driver door open and jumped out, simultaneously grabbing her by her jacket and shoving her behind the truck. "It's bulletproof."

Her spine went to water as the sound of gunfire erupted around them. She froze in place, watching the two men emerge from the desert firing on them. They did look exactly like they were out of a movie. She tried to figure out who they were and if they were in some way connected to Mueen, but the noise was too loud to allow her to piece together the puzzle. And then a burning feeling flashed through her skin, like she'd pressed up against a red-hot iron.

* * *

Goddammit. Why hadn't she just stayed put like he'd asked her to? He couldn't tell what exactly the two men were aiming at until one of them virtually emptied his clip into the side of the trailer.

Amateurs.

Matt used the car door as protection. The targets were so far away, and obviously had better weapons than he did with the range they were getting, but they were firing from the hip, something only thugs did, unconcerned about who they hit.

He shot first at the man on the left. One round missed. Matt adjusted his aim, his heart slowing in time with his deep breaths. With the next round, the man fell to his knees, to get a lower profile. It obviously wasn't as much fun being shot at when you were emptying your clip.

"Is there anyone else with you?" he shouted at Harry. There was no answer.

He ducked and looked around. She was looking back at the trailer. There must be someone in there. "Go get them, get in the car. They're shooting low, I don't want a bullet to go under the car and get you. Okay?"

She nodded.

"After three, I'll give you cover. Okay?" Shit, what was wrong with her? She looked as if she'd seen a ghost.

She nodded back at him again, strangely impassive, blank. Was she going into shock? "Come on, Harry. I need you."

"On three," her reedy voice came back.

That was his girl. "One, two…three." He jumped up and started firing around the two figures, keeping them from advancing. Although, if they got a bit closer, he might have a chance at hitting them. Damn David and the shit weapon he'd loaned him.

He heard the trailer door slam, and seconds later, a fast look revealed Harry reemerged with Mueen at her back. "Get in the car!" he yelled.

Mueen opened the rear door and virtually threw her in the backseat. Matt jumped in the driver seat and revved the engine. He jumped the clutch, and the wheels spun out behind them, spraying sand against the trailer.

"Go that way," Mueen said, pointing through the gap in the seats. It wasn't a pathway he'd been along, but he trusted him to get them to safety in the desert.

As they raced along the path perpendicular to the gunmen, he took a couple of extra shots. Just to make him feel better. And he definitely felt better when the one on the right spun around, arms splayed, with the force of the bullet. *Booyah*.

Within seconds they were out of sight. His mind raced in the knowledge they were safe. Who were they? And who ordered them to take Harry and Mueen out? Or had they only started shooting when he'd arrived? He couldn't remember now. He guessed this meant that the subterfuge, bugs, and rifling through the rooms were over, and the open hostility had begun. He was fine with that. He always did better with an enemy he could see.

"Okay, let me get you guys back to the hotel. We need to figure out who that was and how we can secure the site."

"That won't be possible, I'm afraid." Mueen's voice seemed as soft as the gun he pressed against Matt's neck was hard.

"What the…" Matt began. "Harry? Harry, are you all right?" He tried to look in his mirror, but when he couldn't see her, he tried to turn in his seat. Mueen increased the pressure on his neck.

"Don't tempt me," Mueen said. "I've been wanting to hurt you since you arrived."

Matt couldn't figure him out. He hadn't seemed *that* angry before. Was he just that good of an actor? "Why? What have I ever done to you?"

Mueen laughed deliberately and without humor. In the rearview mirror, Matt saw him swipe at tears in his eyes. Oh, shit. This wasn't going to be good.

"I'm concerned about Harry. Is she okay?"

"She was shot. I think she's going into shock."

"What? You bastard. You fucking…" Matt punched the steering wheel, and Goddammit, he wanted to kill Mueen with his own fucking bare hands. He stomped on the brake. He needed to get out. Needed to see her. Oh, sweet God, please let her be all right. He tried to turn, was afraid to turn and see her. If she died…if he'd somehow not protected her, not kept her safe… His anger and fear swelled in his head until he thought his skull could no longer contain the emotions reeling through his mind.

The gun pressed against his jugular again. "I suggest you keep going. The faster we get to the sheik's home, the faster we can get aid for her."

Matt's breath staggered in and out. Utterly torn between stopping anyway and doing as he was told, he eased his foot back onto the accelerator. Being dead or delaying treatment wouldn't help her at all.

"How long until we get there?" He looked in the rearview mirror and saw that the gun's safety was still on, which he took as a good sign. Even as he thought it he realized he was grasping at straws to find the positive.

"Turn right here," Mueen answered.

There was a crude sign in Arabic staked in the middle of the sandy road. It pointed in the same direction they were headed. He wished he knew what it said.

Chapter 20

When Harry woke, several things hit at the same time. First was a total blank on where she was, and the second was a searing pain in her arm. She struggled to get up from the bed, but the heat that scalded her wound was so bad when she tried to flex the muscle that her brain took a second to register the feeling as extreme pain. When it did, the unfamiliar room started spinning.

While it steadied, she took in her surroundings. She was on a low wooden bed. The white linens were crisp under her touch. Not in an expensive way but in a way that suggested they'd been boiled many times to clean them.

So, there had been a gunfight. Mueen had shoved her in Matt's car virtually at gunpoint. *Oh my God, Matt.* What had Mueen done to him? The last thing she remembered was lying in the backseat and a gunshot echoing around the car. Her heart clenched in unbearable fear. Her fingers dug into the sheets as she bowed her head, almost unable to muster the strength to raise it again. Dry sobs racked through her body. Her soul spiraled down through the dusty floor of the room. He was dead because of her.

Because she'd refused to leave, a determination that had partially been caused by her certainty that Danny's friend wouldn't leave her alone in Iraq. She was selfish. She'd risked his life like it had been hers to risk. She'd never cared if *she* died, but now…

She unwound the fingers of one hand from the sheets and placed them gently on her wound, pink through the bandage. She pressed, and a wave of nausea pulsed through her body. She pushed again, harder, and all she felt was pain. A white-hot, all-encompassing pain. No thought. No worry. No grief, just pain. Beautiful, unthinking pain.

The door of the room slammed open. "Harry! What are you— stop it! You're hurting yourself!" Hands grabbed her and wrenched her fingers away from her bandage.

"Molly?" she whispered. "I'm dreaming…" She fell backward onto the pillow. "A nightmare…"

* * *

When she opened her eyes again, Molly was sitting right next to the bed, intently staring at her. "Are you okay now?" she asked pressing a cool, wet cloth against Harry's forehead.

"I had a dream…" She looked down at her arm again and squeezed her eyes shut as the grief overtook her again.

"It wasn't a dream, sugar. You really got shot. Well, a ricochet we think. But you're safe now. Mueen says—"

"No!" she tried to yell, but a whisper came out instead. "He held us at gunpoint. Matt…" Tears trickled down her face, and she turned away from Molly.

"I know, honey, I know. Don't worry, though…"

The words barely registered with Harry. Everything was wrong. She was shot in Iraq. Where Danny died. Where Matt died. Molly was on a plane back home. She couldn't be here. Although…she couldn't be sure where here was. It was too much. Too much. She wished she could disappear. Like she never existed. She took a deep breath…

> She was in the car again; this time she could see what was happening. Matt was shooting out the window. She tried to say something, but the noise was so loud, and Mueen pressed a gun muzzle against her stomach. Then he pressed it against Matt's neck and pulled the trigger. She smelled the gunpowder, the noise disorientated her, and Matt disappeared into a fine pink mist in front of her eyes.
>
> She screamed. "Matt. Matt. Where are you? Where did you go? Matt!"

Harry snapped upright in the bed, suddenly awake, heart pumping. Molly was still there, eyes wide in surprise. "It's okay," she said quietly. But behind the bedroom door a voice replied, "Harry? Harry!"

"Matt?" she whispered.

Molly frowned. "He can't come in here. Only women can—"

* * *

He'd been waiting for the damned sheik for hours. He wasn't allowed to see Harry, and had only been told that she was doing okay. Molly, whose flight had been canceled, had been picked up, too, and was tending to her. He didn't know what to make of the situation, but his training told him to keep calm and keep everyone important to him within sight, or at least within calling distance.

No one seemed as if they were itching to harm them, to be fair, but he'd seen too many smiling, friendly-seeming people watch as Humvees were blown up by IEDs they'd placed.

To make this epic fuckup even more fucked-up, there'd been no bullet holes on the Suburban. Not one scuff. It made no sense. That man on the right who'd been shooting at them, there was no way he could have missed the car. With the number of rounds he'd dropped, the entire side of the car should have been riddled with bullet craters. Nada. Not a thing.

And yet the guy on the left had managed to pepper the trailer with enough lead that it would be permanently air conditioned.

His response to the uncertainty of his situation was to pace. He'd paced for over an hour, with Mueen watching his every move. Damned if he was going to say anything to him. He could just watch and be bored to death. Hopefully.

After a while, he sat. His skin was crawling with the idea that Harry needed him and he wasn't allowed to see her. He put his face in his hands and tried to make sense of the past few days.

And then he heard her screams for him. His subconscious threw him into auto pilot. He was going to her. He didn't care who he had to kill or maim to achieve that goal. There was nothing that would keep him from her. Gender rules be damned. He jumped up from the sack of coffee beans he'd been relaxing on and stepped toward Mueen.

"Don't make me hurt you—I'm going to her, and you can try to stop me if you like, but it won't be pretty. And neither will you." His fists clenched, ready to beat the bastard to a pulp if necessary, but instead, Mueen's lips quirked up, and he stood aside with an amused look in his eyes.

Matt ran to the corridor that he knew led to the women's quarters. At the end were two guards, sitting at a table playing cards for matchsticks. They stood as soon as they saw him, and one pulled out a knife. Knife? It was more like a small scythe. That's why Mueen had let him pass. Well, more fool him.

He knew they took the virtue of the resident women very seriously, but a man with a baby-machete was not going to stop him from getting to Harry. The guard without the knife took a swing at him, which he ducked easily, delivering a fast uppercut to his solar plexus. The man gasped for breath and fell backward over his chair. Not so well trained, obviously.

The knife man grinned, showing a mouth of a full three teeth. Matt mentally gave him three seconds to make his move otherwise he was going straight through him. He got to two before the man stepped in, turning his side to Matt, and stabbed at him with the knife. Sweet hell. He even held one arm behind his back like he was a musketeer.

Oh, how he wanted to just pull out a gun and shoot him, but they'd stripped him of all his weapons when they arrived. He'd been worried that if he protested it would delay Harry's treatment.

Instead he ran toward the man, knocking his knife hand out of the way. As the knife clattered to the floor, Matt punched him one time in the jaw. A "knockout punch" they'd called it in unarmed combat training. It worked every time. There was a tap on his shoulder, and he turned, just in time for Mueen to punch him in the head. The bastard's ring dug into his head, but he kept his wits about him and spun, whipping his legs out from under him. Mueen fell, whacking his own head against the wall. He went limp.

Matt ran toward her room and smashed it open.

Chapter 21

Harry's eyes remained on the door. An abrupt, loud clattering sound came from the other side. Grunts. Things falling over. The door exploded open, banging against the wall behind it. It was Matt. He stood in the doorway, blood dripping from the side of his head.

Tears flooded her eyes, so much so that she couldn't see him properly. "You're alive?" Harry jumped up, oblivious to the pain in her arm, and flung herself into his arms. He enveloped her in his huge frame, and she was home.

"Of course I am." He pulled away from her and looked into her eyes. "Why did you think I wasn't?"

"Mueen. He had a gun, pointed at your neck. And I couldn't remember any more…" except the dream where he blew up. "I had a dream, I think, and I saw you explode when he shot you." She couldn't help her bottom lip from shaking, but it had been a dream. Somehow, because everyone in EOD talked about the "pretty pink mist" when someone is blown up by a bomb, she had always seen that image after Danny died. And now she was dreaming about Matt exploding in the same way that Danny had.

"Aw, sweetheart. It's okay..." He pulled her back into his arms, and she laid her head against his chest.

Molly eased out of the room slowly, shutting the door behind her.

"Are you okay?" he asked, pushing her away a little and examining her face and body. He took in the basic white bandage that covered her wound. "I think it was a ricochet from a bullet that hit the side of the trailer." He let a finger gently stroke her over the bandage.

"Mueen?" she asked, sniffing and sitting back on the bed. "He held me at gunpoint." Her body felt as if it didn't belong to her. She was numb. Not even her arm hurt. She could have died there. And the thought of that wasn't acceptable. For the first time in many years, she felt herself reacting to a near-death experience with fear. And the implications of that fear were too much for her to even examine in her head.

"Yup. Me too. I hit him pretty hard, though." His tone suggested pride in his actions.

A smile touched her lips for a second. "Good. What happened, I mean, why? Where are we?"

"We're at the sheik's home." He looked around the room and shrugged. "I think, anyway."

"That's good, I think. At least he saved me from the police last night." A huge yawn came over her. "God, I'm so sleepy."

"Lie down," Matt said softly. "We'll talk about it when you wake up."

"Stay with me?" she asked, eyes already closed.

He nodded, and she slipped back under the covers. Matt was here. Everything was fine. Matt and Molly were okay. She was alive...

* * *

Right here. She wanted to stay right here. Warm, protected, safe...Right here forever. Except...no. She jerked awake. It hadn't been a dream.

Or, some of it had been a dream. Matt's head was on the pillow next to hers, except he was fully dressed and on top of the covers. Somehow she had snuggled next to him and slept beneath his arm. She took a deep breath, taking in his soapy scent.

Fully alert, she shifted up on to her good elbow. Her other arm had dulled to an ache. Crap. Matt still had blood on his face. She'd forgotten that he'd burst into the room injured. What a selfish, self-absorbed bitch she was. A cursory glance told her that there was nothing in the room she could use to clean up his cut.

She peered down at him wondering what to do with him. This, *they*, had started as fun, a diversion. But she couldn't go through this again. She couldn't allow herself this closeness. The agony that had invaded her when she thought he had died was the same agony she felt when Danny had died. A painful void inside her. A vacuum of terror. She wasn't going to do that again. She'd promised herself. She was too scared of what she might do if she was hurt that way again. Too scared of the emptiness. It had taken her four years to get over the pain and grief of losing Danny. She wasn't sure she was strong enough to go through that again. And yet what she had felt when she thought Matt was dead was just as powerful as before. However well she'd hidden her heart, Matt had gotten close enough to be able to hurt it. She was as scared about that as she was at being shot at.

She thought back to the last time they had shared a bed...just the night before, even though so much seemed to have happened since then. She'd known that was dangerous. His easy intimacy, drawing her into an intimacy she couldn't afford. After Danny, how could she allow herself to get involved with someone in the military again, especially someone in harm's way? Just no. She couldn't lose anyone else that she cared about. She couldn't live through that again.

She extricated herself from his arm, got up, and backed away slowly.

"What's wrong?" he said, a deep frown creasing his forehead and opening up the cut. Blood dripped down his face. "You look like you've seen a ghost."

"I...what? Nothing. You're bleeding," she said, and reached for a corner of bedsheet. When it wouldn't reach his face, and Matt wouldn't move, she shrugged and dropped it.

"I know. Your friend Mueen hit me."

Harry sat on the bed. "What's going on? How did Molly get here? Is she with Mueen?" A coldness wafted over her, and she dragged a blanket from the bed around her. All the people she trusted were firmly in a questionable category. Except for Matt. And he was in a whole new category now. Except when they got through this, she knew exactly what she was going to do with him. She was going to walk away from him. *Had* to walk away from him.

"Don't start getting paranoid. Molly's flight was canceled, so Mueen picked her up again and brought her here to us. She doesn't know what's going on, either. None of us do, really."

"Well it's about time we found out. I can't deal with this. I want to know what's going on, and I want to know now."

"I can tell you they really didn't want me in the women's quarters," Matt said, wiping the blood from his face.

"No kidding," she said, her mouth twitching into a smile of its own accord. "Are we here under duress, then? I mean, are we kidnapped?" She didn't feel kidnapped, but that didn't mean anything.

Mueen knocked and opened the door, not going in, but hovering in the doorway.

"I guess we should ask the source," Matt said. "Can we leave, or are we being kept as prisoners here?"

"No. You are free to go. I just would not recommend it." Mueen shifted his weight from foot to foot. "The men in black are patrolling the site. It will be difficult to get past them back to the hotel."

"Forgive me if I don't necessarily accept your recommendations," Matt snarled.

"His Highness will be back soon, and he will tell you what he knows. Perhaps." He half sneered at Matt.

"Mueen, I don't understand," Harry said softly into the room that had suddenly become tense with testosterone.

He hesitated and looked at them one by one. "I'm sorry, I did not mean to alarm you. I was told to get you here as soon as possible. For your safety. I was worried that you wouldn't come unless...encouraged. His Highness is buying information for you. For us." He held his hand out to one side, and Ain stepped into his arm.

"Ain. What are you doing here? Are you all right?" Harry said, standing up.

"We're all very well." She turned to her husband. "He's back. Let's go to the living quarters and hear what His Highness has to say."

* * *

The sheik was nothing at all like Matt had expected. Nothing, really nothing. It rendered him virtually speechless.

An older man, maybe fifty, sat in a corner armchair in a much more formal room than Matt had seen so far in the house. He wore an old but still sharp-looking three-piece suit with red socks and Oxfords. The man smiled and jumped out of his chair as they came in. Matt gauged he was maybe five and a half feet tall. But the power he wielded was undeniable.

"Ms. Markowitz. It is a real pleasure to meet you."

Harry beamed. "It's an honor to meet you at last, Your Highness. Thank you so much for facilitating our work"—her face fell—"well…"

"I know, I know. Well, we shall see what we can do to fix your problems, shall we?"

"This is Matt Stanning…" Harry said.

Matt held out his hand to the sheik, who gripped it firmly.

"You are the air force man," the sheik stated.

Matt took a second as his mind whirred. It was way too late to be covert, he guessed. "Yes, sir."

The sheik glanced at Mueen, who shifted uncomfortably and looked away. Matt wondered if Mueen had told him about his animosity toward Matt.

"Hmmm. Interesting." The sheik said, and then Harry was introducing him to Molly.

When they had all settled in chairs, the sheik smiled and looked at Matt. "I see you are confused by my appearance, yes? You were expecting some kind of Omar Sharif character from *Lawrence of Arabia*, weren't you?"

"I suppose I was," he replied. "Actually, I didn't know what to expect."

"I was educated in England until I was eighteen. Eton, actually. When I returned to help my father with his community duties, I brought some Western sensibilities with me, as my father hoped I would. I find when I meet with the chief of police, dressing like this causes him some discomfort, which I like to use to my advantage."

"What exactly does a sheik do?" Molly asked, and Matt looked in amusement as Harry winced. But the sheik's eyes wrinkled up as he looked at Molly and smiled.

"I look after the people who live in my region, get work for them"—he nodded gently in Harry's direction—"make sure families have enough food, settle disputes between neighbors, which thankfully are few. I liken my position to being the head-master at Eton, or any school. I try to keep the peace, I look out for the people, and I protect them from harm if I can."

"He is a great leader," Ain said, bowing her head slightly.

The sheik said nothing but beamed at her. Matt got the feeling he was a man they could trust, even though it didn't really matter—they didn't really have a choice.

"What did the police say?" Matt asked.

The sheik became solemn. "I'm afraid to say that your colleague Professor Rapson was indeed murdered. He was shot in the stomach. The police believe that he interrupted a thief. His staff say that his briefcase is missing.

"Um…" Harry bit her lip. "I have his satchel. Could that be what they mean?"

"How did you happen by that?" the sheik asked evenly.

"We were having dinner when he went back up to his room to get some papers to show me. He left his bag with me. And, oh God. I left it in my bedroom. If anyone searches my room and finds it, won't they think I had something to do with his death?" She stuck her thumbnail between her teeth and looked at Matt worriedly.

The sheik inclined his head slightly to Mueen, who left the room. Matt wondered what they were doing. Maybe they didn't believe Harry's story. Although Matt suddenly remembered that Mueen was also at the hotel that night.

He was about to speak up, when Mueen came back in.

"I've sent someone to get the bag, if it's still there." He nodded at the sheik.

"Very well, Mueen, my son. Maybe, because you and I know what this is all about, you should, perhaps, tell your story to our visitors."

Mueen nearly choked on his own tongue, and Matt sat forward, interested in anything that would cause him this amount of discomfort.

"Very well," the sheik said, settling back in his chair. "Maybe your wife would start with her story?"

Chapter 22

Ain took Mueen's hand and nodded at the sheik. Harry wondered what kind of story would have them both looking so sick.

"It was a June evening ten years ago. A beautiful evening. My family and I had eaten at a Bedouin settlement, close to the site you are working at. We were wishing our hosts farewell, when we heard a boom, like a firework.

"I remember thinking that it was a perfect night for fireworks, warm and still, with a bright moon. But as we looked for the display, the sound of an aircraft got closer and closer. Unusually low. We couldn't see anything in the sky, until it was over us." She laughed softly. "I was so scared. I felt that if I reached up, I could have touched it.

"But although there had been no fighting here, we knew the country was at war. There was another bang, and it seemed as if half of the airplane fell away with sparks. Then there was silence until the sound of the plane as it hit the sand." Ain rubbed her arms as if the memory of the night was giving her goose bumps. It was certainly giving Harry goose bumps, that was for sure.

"The Bedouin leaders rode camels to get to the wreckage.

Some of the younger people there took old motorbikes, and my father and I took our truck. I prayed for there to be survivors. I prayed harder than I ever had before."

Matt leaned forward. "What kind of plane was it?"

"It was a military plane. I don't know the type." She looked at Mueen questioningly.

"It was a C-130," he said, looking at the floor.

"All I could tell was that it had a small American flag on its tail," Ain continued. "By the time my father and I arrived, two men in uniform had been taken out—and were lying on the sand."

Matt swallowed visibly. "Dead?"

"Alive. Just," Ain said.

Matt sat back in his chair, a disbelieving look on his face.

Harry wondered what was going through his head. Maybe that Ain could tell him where they buried the bodies, and then, maybe his mission would be complete.

"His Highness arrived at the scene when we did. He gave orders to everyone. Our orders, my father and mine, were to take the men in our truck back to our house."

"Oh my God, Ain. You saw the men? I came looking for them. So I can bring them home to their families," Matt said.

Harry felt tears well in her eyes when she saw Matt's glisten with the recognition that he would in fact be bringing his troops home at last.

Mueen sat back in his chair, eyes averted from everyone.

Ain continued. "We loaded them into the backseat of the truck, and brought them home to the village. The medical woman was called and we kept them both alive for one day. They both had broken legs and crushed ribs, and the older man had at least one puncture in his lung from his broken ribs.

"I tried really hard to save them both." Tears were falling down Ain's face unchecked. "I really did."

"Thank you. Thank you so much for trying." Matt took her hand and squeezed it. "It means the world to me that someone took care of them."

"And to me," Harry said, trying hard not to cry herself. She wondered if Ain telling her story was cathartic or if it amplified the emotion for her.

"He died the following morning. There was nothing we could do. The journey to the nearest functioning hospital that wasn't under Hussein's power was just too far. We knew if we tried to take them anywhere, they would be captured and probably left to die. We…I thought it better they die with us than with the president's soldiers. I still don't know if I made the right choice for him. I think about it every day."

Him? Surely she meant "them"? Wait…Harry looked at Matt to see if he'd realized what she'd said.

"What about the other one?" Harry said gently, pieces of the puzzle falling together like they were magnetic.

"He woke up three weeks later. He didn't know his name, or how he'd got to our house. He couldn't walk, and I was the only one in the village who spoke English at the time. For months I looked after him, we talked, I taught him Arabic, and as his memory gradually came back, we…"

"Fell in love," Mueen said, raising his eyes for the first time. He looked directly at Matt, who was shaking his head.

"What's your name?" Matt asked softly.

"Captain Douglas Carpelli from Pittsburgh, Pennsylvania," Mueen said.

Harry suddenly realized why he sounded so American to her sometimes. She blew air out from her cheeks incredulously. Wow.

"You didn't make contact with anyone?" Matt asked. "Once you'd recovered?"

"I wanted to, but no one came for me. For us. Do you understand?" Mueen held his gaze unapologetically. "No one came."

* * *

Matt did understand. The military hadn't sent anyone to help them, to try to find them. The money-moving operation was off-the-books, a black op. The military credo, across all branches of service, was leave no one behind. It was unthinkable that the organization he'd dedicated his life to had elected to leave the airmen there, in the middle of a war.

"But it was your duty…" Matt began, relentlessly trying to pin the blame on anyone but the military. But as the words came out, he knew he couldn't blame Mueen for his actions.

"My duty was to safeguard the package until it got into the right hands. If I fell into enemy hands, my only duty was to serve honorably and keep my mouth shut."

"And he did. He hid the container as soon as we found it, and he to this day has never told me what was in it," Ain said.

Matt paced the room. "You are still a member of the United States armed forces and you must—"

Mueen shouted, "In that case, call me sir. I outrank you and won't be spoken to like that."

Matt opened his mouth to shout back but realized he was right. He couldn't have it both ways: either he was a civilian who would take orders from Matt, if necessary, or he was a captain, and dammit, Matt would have to take orders from him. He gave a short laugh and shook his head. "Fair point."

In essence the captain was a deserter. But what was he supposed to have done in the middle of a desert, injured with no rescue on its way? What would he have done? From his file, he knew that the captain had no family to go back to…Who was he to judge? He looked at the couple in the center of the room. And then at Harry. Well, he couldn't blame Carpelli for falling in love; after all, that's exactly what he'd done himself. He swiped a hand through his hair. *Shit on a stick*. What had he just admitted to?

"Do you know what was in your container?" Matt asked him.

"Both the sheik and I know," the captain said.

"If you know, why haven't either of you done anything with the money?" Matt was amazed, and looked between the captain and the sheik incredulously.

"Wait a minute. Back up," Molly said. "What money?"

Harry briefed her as succinctly as she could and then nodded at Carpelli to carry on.

"I didn't know what it was for, or *who* it was for. Also, the container was rigged to blow if anyone tampered with it. The sheik and I thought it better buried and forgotten."

"Rigged to blow?" Matt mentally rubbed his hands together at the thought of eyeing explosives again. A thread of adrenaline spiked from the top of his spine down his back.

"Charges were attached to both sides of the container. Tech Sergeant Ranger was trying to secure the pallet in some bad clear-air turbulence when one of them detonated. He died instantly." Mueen looked down at his hands as he flipped beads around a thick string. "And that blew a hole in the fuselage, precipitating our landing."

Matt thought his head was going to explode. He couldn't believe that no one was tasked with trying to find them. But since no one had reported the aircraft as missing, how could they search for them? He also couldn't believe that someone rigged cargo in a fucking aircraft to blow. After his initial outrage that the captain hadn't tried to get back to base, he kind of empathized with him.

The sheik spoke into the silence. "So now all our cards are on the table, you should know that Americans in big black cars have been patrolling both the professor's and your sites. The chief of police told me that he had fast-tracked some visas for twenty men arriving tomorrow. For"—he pulled out a piece of paper from his breast pocket—"MGL Security."

The sheik had underlined the letters MGL, and Matt's mind instantly went back to Rapson's papers. His Megellin papers all had underlined letters. He thought they'd been doodles, but no. Rapson had underlined the M, the G, and the L in the name Megellin. Goddammit. Could Megellin just be a front for MGL Security?

"So we have only today to stop that money falling into the hands of MGL. Okay, who's in?" Matt said, only half joking.

Harry and Molly stuck up their hands immediately, followed by Carpelli.

Matt looked at them all with their earnest faces...well, not Carpelli's. His face was as impassive as ever.

Matt took a deep breath and released it. *Okay, then.* "Do you have a sat phone I can use?" Matt asked the sheik. There was silence for a second, and Matt wondered for a moment if they really were prisoners.

The sheik nodded to Mueen, and he in turn nodded at Matt to follow him. They walked down a parallel corridor to the women's quarters. This one had just one guard. Matt winced when he realized it was baby-knife man. He smiled broadly at him as they went past.

"I always thought you hated me from the moment you saw me," Matt said.

"I did. I was worried for my future if you saw me for what I was, and worried for anyone who found and tried to tamper with the payload. I'm still really fucking pissed at the air force for leaving me here. And worried you'd drag me back Stateside. Yeah, you could say I hated you." He paused. "Are you going to?"

"Take you back? Hell if I know," Matt replied, honestly.

Mueen opened the door to what was clearly the sheik's office. "Does it need to be secure?"

"Not really. I think the odds of them tapping the sheik's phone, or the person I'm going to contact, are remote at best."

"Then, here"—he threw a phone the size of a book at Matt—"This is what we have."

"Wow. You are rocking the eighties here, aren't you?"

Mueen rolled his eyes and sat in an old, battered armchair.

"You're not going to give me any privacy?" Matt's finger hesitated over the button.

"Nope." He tapped his fingers on the arm of the chair. "We don't have all day."

Matt took a slip of paper from his wallet. First rule of travel: have everyone's personal phone numbers on hand. He dialed his commander.

He picked up after two rings. "Jenks."

Matt couldn't help but feel a little relieved when he heard his voice. "It's Stanning, sir."

"Thank God. I've given the team travel orders to get to your location, but with the official visas they have to get, it may be a week before you see them."

Dammit. A week would definitely be too late. Whatever was

in the crate might already be in the wrong hands. "Then I may need to...act without them."

"I realize that." There was silence.

"Do you know for sure what is in the crate?" Matt asked.

"As we suspected," he said, obviously trying to be discreet over the phone. "As soon as I sent your travel orders, I started receiving phone calls asking where you were and what you were doing. Initially I just told them what I knew. That some archaeologist had found parts of a military plane in Iraq. Then I decided to keep quiet about where you were. I figured you'd do better by yourself. Was I right?"

"That's yet to be seen. But you did get MGL Security to provide me with a security detail, right?"

"Who, son?"

Matt wondered if the connection was bad. "MGL Security?" A sinking feeling pitted his stomach as he waited through the silence at the other end of the phone.

"No. I didn't tell anyone you were there. I was too worried about the talk going around as it was. You know how many troops get out of the service and go straight into private security contractors? All those people have a direct line back into the military. If you've been approached by anyone from MGL..." His commander's voice sounded strange.

"I have, but it was an ex-colleague of mine. I can deal with him. Sir, can you do some digging and see what kind of links MGL has to other companies or organizations operating here in Iraq?" He had a suspicion that the answer would be the Megellin Foundation. It had gotten to the stage where he almost hoped it was. It would make the most sense and take a big unknown from their equation.

"I will do that, Stanning. I'll get word to you as soon as I can.

Listen…" he said lowering his voice. "They've tasked satellites over your position there. Both internal and external. An old buddy in the NSA told me. The government and…other interests are using private satellites to gather intelligence. All of a sudden, everyone's up to their necks in requests for pictures of your site to see what's going on. All I can do is tell you when they're going to be live. When they're overhead."

"Roger that, sir. Thank you. Get back to me as soon as you know." He pressed a button to hang up. *Shit*. And yet a plan was formulating in his head. One that almost persuaded him to smile.

"So?" Mueen said, getting up.

"My ex-colleague, David, was less about having my six, and more about keeping tabs on me." He could tell him his suspicions, but he couldn't help still think of him as Mueen, instead of Captain Carpelli.

"Assuming we can get our hands on the money before anyone else, if you know anyone who can help get it into the right hands, and they have their own passports rather than official ones, the sheik can get them in-country without visas," Mueen said as they loaded the equipment into the truck by the tents. "If they have personal passports, it won't be a problem as long as we had a few hours' notice to grease the right palms."

"When you say 'the right hands,' I'm guessing you don't mean the United States Treasury," Matt said.

"I can use Google as well as the next person. Harry was right. The money belongs here. To build schools, and hospitals."

Matt sighed. His black-and-white view on obeying orders was becoming more and more gray. "Why can't you use the sheik's men?" he asked.

"He doesn't want to put temptation in their hands," he replied.

"If anyone were to take off with the money instead of delivering it to the agreed regions, His Highness would be duty bound to find and punish those people, and he really doesn't have the stomach for that."

"I get that. There's only one group of people I trust with something like that," Matt said. "I think it's time to put the band back together. Let me make one more call and then we can go find the others. I think it's time to tell everyone what we know."

Chapter 23

While Matt was briefing them, coming clean on everything he knew, or suspected, Harry wondered how long he'd known about these things and been keeping them from her. It pissed her off to imagine he'd deliberately been keeping information close to his chest. If he'd been trying to protect her...

In the middle of explaining about MGL, he put his head in his hands and groaned. What was wrong with him? She looked at everyone else, who seemed equally concerned. Then he jumped up and started pacing.

"Matt? What is it?" Harry asked.

He stopped moving and looked at them all in silence as if making up his mind what to tell them. Harry scowled at him.

"It's David. I just remembered something. Just after Malcolm was killed, he took me to his hotel, and while we were talking, he referred to him as 'the old man.'"

There was silence in the room. Molly raised her hand and said, "I'm sorry. I don't get it."

"He'd never met Rapson. How would he know that he was an old man?"

There was silence in the room. Harry couldn't believe that one of Danny and Matt's friends was a bad guy, someone who would kill a harmless old man. As far as she remembered, all the old EOD boys had been thick as thieves. An ironic expression, now that she thought about it.

"We need a plan to get that money before Megellin-MGL Security do, and to make sure it gets back to the people who need it. I can't bear the thought of an American company getting their hands on the Iraqi people's money and...basically, I don't really care about anything else now. No disrespect to your story," she said, looking at Mueen.

"None taken. But there's no point having a plan to distribute the money if we don't have a plan to actually get the money and keep MGL away from it."

"They have my maps," Harry said. "I'm sorry I didn't think about it before, but I'd realized they were missing from the laptop case just before we started getting shot at. Someone took them from my room, probably the same time Malcolm..."

Matt squeezed her hand, and the warmth settled her heart, made her feel protected. She fisted her other hand. No. She can't let this happen. She couldn't allow herself to rely on anyone else for comfort or...anything. She gently pulled her hand away from his.

"The map wasn't plotted accurately, but it had the ballpark location of the geo-phys results. And—" *Crap*. She'd left her actual laptop in the trailer, too. "My laptop with all the exact coordinates is in the trailer. It's password protected, but..."

"No password will be too much of a problem for a professional military security firm." Matt nodded pensively, and then he straightened and gazed at them with the air of a commander. "I have a plan. We need to get out there. We need to move before they bring in their reinforcements. We need to secure that money."

* * *

The call came about three hours later. Jenks had told him that the satellite does a full rotation around the earth every ninety minutes. To task it to exactly the right spot would take a little longer. They had two hours and twenty-three minutes to get everything ready. Matt had gotten everything in order, and he just hoped he'd thought of everything. David and Maggie, his ex–Military Intelligence friend, were the only two rogue elements to his plan. He set the timer on his watch. Really, they needed everything and everyone in place about five minutes before that. He'd just have to manage as best as he could.

This is what he lived for. How had he stayed in JPAC for so long? It fulfilled him like no other job had, but he had finally figured out that his brain and body worked better when he was neck-deep in shit. Plans and puzzles were clearer when adrenaline bathed his system in a wash of vitality. He didn't regret a day he'd spent reuniting military families with their fallen heroes. But this was where he needed to be. If only for his own benefit. He hadn't felt this alive since his EOD work before Danny died. It was like he'd been given a new lease on his professional life. And he intended to use that lease to its fullest.

Matt, Harry, Molly, and Mueen had all left in one vehicle to the staging area the sheik had arranged for them. He'd given a list of things he'd needed to Mueen, and he had miraculously procured all of them within a space of a couple of hours. Fuck if he knew what he was going to do about him. That was a question for later. If they managed to pull this off. The odds were stacked against them, but he was nothing if not determined. He looked around the truck. They all looked determined and excited. Talk about ragtag group of misfits: a combat airman, an archaeologist, a grad student, and a deserter. If he could have left the women at the house, he would have. But he needed them there.

He let Mueen drive, since he was Matt's operations guy. Which was amusing in itself. Besides which, he seemed to be able to navigate the dunes and roads that had few if any distinguishing features. Also they had to arrive perpendicular to the staging area that the sheik had pulled strings to organize. To whoever was at Harry's site, in the distance, all they would see was what would look like a series of Bedouin tents. They could arrive in the black Suburban without being seen.

Mueen slowed right down as they approached the tents, so as not to leave a trail of sand dust in the air. They got out of the truck quietly and slipped into the tent structure. It was empty of people, but they'd been provided food and water, as well as guns and ammo. Not good guns and ammo, but what looked like whatever they'd been able to collect in the last few decades. Some of the actions were rusty and unusable. Matt and Mueen got to figuring out which ones they could use.

"Please try to not kill anyone," Molly said as she sat next to Harry and watched them check magazines and safeties.

Mueen ignored her, but Matt looked up. "That's not the primary objective, obviously, but I hope you would rather we came back alive than they came for you alive?"

"Sure, sure," she answered in a quiet voice.

"I think what she means is try not to shoot first and ask questions later," Harry said, a frown furrowing her brow.

"You want the money, or do you want MGL to have the money?" he asked as he was slipping mags into his pockets.

She just stared at his orneriness, but he couldn't help that. Not today. And God only knew if they had a tomorrow. His plan was…well, ballsy, and almost certain to fail unless all the moving parts worked exactly as he planned, which in real life was almost always never. But if they did have a tomorrow, he was going to get her, and keep her, come hell or high water.

Yeah, when this was all over… *Crap*, he couldn't be distracted like this. *Mind on the game, Stanning.* He checked his watch. They had an hour now. No time to waste.

"You all ready?"

Molly and Harry nodded eagerly.

"Then let's roll."

Chapter 24

Mueen had found the two-car patrol riding up the mile or so that accounted for both Harry's and Malcolm's sites. They stayed on the boundary road, and Matt guessed they'd been given orders not to disturb the sites.

Five of them walked to the site. The four of them plus one man leading a camel. It was the perfect camouflage; they were all dressed as Bedouins, or at least as Mueen said, how Westerners would expect them to look.

As they drew closer to Harry's site, Matt nodded at her. When they passed the trailer, hiding them from the eyeline of the patrol, she and Molly peeled off and hid behind the trailer. Their mission was to retrieve the laptop, if it was still there. As they slowed next to the trailer, the extra man the sheik had provided pulled down their equipment from the camel and stacked it behind the trailer.

Mueen and Matt were going to neutralize the patrol one car at a time. That was the tricky part. It would be very obvious to the other car that one had stopped patrolling. But dressed as they were, they should be able to get close enough to at least get them to stop without seeming like a threat.

In order for Matt's crazy plan to work, they had less than an hour to get everything prepared.

Matt checked his watch. "Ready to go, captain?"

"Roger that." Mueen took the camel from his friend, and in a low voice told him to get back to the tents and wait for them. Mueen took a look at Matt as if they weren't entirely sure they would make it back to the tents. Matt just grinned.

"Gotta go balls to the wall or go home," he said to the pilot.

"Easy for you to say," Mueen grumbled. "Here we go." They were approaching the first black Suburban.

Matt stood in its way, with his head down. The driver sounded his horn but stopped, thanks no doubt to the camel. It was one thing to run down a man, a totally other thing to hit a camel.

Maneuvering the camel to hide his reach for the gun attached to the camel's harness, Mueen went up to the vehicle as if to talk to them. While their attention was on Mueen, Matt ducked under the camel's legs, and crouched down, he dug his knife into the Suburban's front tire. He had to get them out of there because there was no other way to neutralize people in a bullet-proof car. As soon as he was sure that the tire was deflating, he moved the camel, shielding himself from the car with it. Both Mueen and he walked past the vehicle slowly, watching as it tried to take off. If it had been on a road, it could have still driven well enough, but in sand, it was nonresponsive.

Matt slapped the camel on its behind, and it took off loping back toward the tents. Both men got out of the car, neither of them checking that Mueen and Matt had really walked past. Clumsy operatives. Matt shucked off his robe and pulled his weapon in front of him.

"Hey, guys?" he said.

They spun around, both reaching for their sidearms; one had his, and the other had an empty holster. Obviously he'd left it in the car, because Mueen had slipped in the open door and was waving it.

"Drop it," Matt said calmly, pointing his weapon at the man who spat something in an unknown language at him.

The man dropped his weapon and put his hands on his head without Matt having to ask him. Nice.

"Company." Mueen said.

Dammit. He was hoping it would take them a minute or so longer to realize something was going down with the other vehicle.

Before he could respond, the man with the beard and the sneer bent at the waist, placed his hands on the sand, and flung a foot out that missed Matt's head by less than an inch but kicked the gun out of his hand. It had happened so fast, Matt had only managed to move that inch out of his way by leaning back, otherwise he'd probably have been unconscious as well as unarmed. Fuck that shit. Gun was out of reach, but then so was the other guy's.

The man came at him with straight arms, like he was swinging swords, and it took Matt back a second. What the hell was he doing? Then as one of the guy's forearms smashed into his face, he realized that the man had heavy-duty metal arm guards on. Light flashed in his eyes as his brain exploded under the blow. It was as if he'd been hit by a crowbar.

He lay dazed for a second before attempting to get up. The sun-bleached sand shifted and swirled around him. He managed to get on his hands and knees, but knew that if he didn't get up, this was a perfect target for a...

The man kicked him hard in his ribs, and he went down again.

This time he managed to roll under the Suburban, frustrating the foreign guy's attempts at kicking him again.

He couldn't see what Mueen was doing. He took a few breaths to try to eliminate the weird patterns of light in his eyes that were making it difficult to see anything. He rolled out the other side of the car before Iron Arms could find his gun again. He opened his eyes to see a black-clad man falling. He rolled again fast to avoid the man crashing on top of him. Mueen had delivered the same knockout punch that Matt had done on him.

"Get up, man. Stop dicking around. The other patrol is here," Mueen said, offering a hand. Matt took it, not bothering to explain that he wasn't hiding under the vehicle just for fun.

Gunshots erupted around them. Sand flew up as they dived behind the Suburban. "Are we allowed to shoot first and ask questions later if it's clear they are?" Mueen asked.

"Okay by me," Matt said, looking for his weapon. Mueen checked the clip in his. Then Matt looked into the car and laughed. No shit. He opened the truck, giving them an even bigger bulletproof shield. "Look."

Like some good Suburban minivan, the trunk space had dividers so things wouldn't roll around the back. Within each divider were guns. Lots of guns. With ammo. Mueen looked at his revolver and chucked it on the sand. He reached in for a SIG Sauer and checked the mag. "I might just love these guys," Mueen said, sticking another under his waistband.

"They are certainly prepared for some kind of zombie apocalypse, that's for sure," Matt said, taking an M16 rifle.

There was a lull in the shooting. Car doors slammed. Okay, they were getting out of the car. Stupid, really stupid, but good for them. Matt checked his watch again. This might work.

He peeked out from behind the car, wishing he could open

the side doors to get a bit more cover. Fuck. It was Maggie and David. He needed this to work, but he didn't know if he could shoot in cold blood people he knew, regardless of their level of treachery.

"What's the matter?" Mueen whispered.

"It's David and Maggie."

Mueen didn't reply.

Matt took another look to see how close they were. Maggie shot at him, skimming the paintwork of the truck inches from his face. Yeah, he probably shouldn't have pissed her off at breakfast.

David was shooting, too, but didn't seem to be making contact. He was behind Maggie, who seemed hell-bent on making them both dead. Matt rolled around to the other side of the truck to see David better. He seemed to be laughing. And then he waved at Matt.

"What the…?"

David leveled his weapon and shot. It made a noise, but nothing hit the truck. Then he laughed again and pointed his weapon at Maggie and shot at her.

Maggie kept shooting toward the rear of the car.

Matt stood away from the car so that David could see him but Maggie couldn't. He was still laughing. He shot at Matt again, then pointed the weapon at his own head and fired. Nothing. He'd been firing blanks, but his mag must be empty of even those. Suddenly the unscuffed Suburban from the morning made sense.

Maggie looked back at David for a second, and he straightened his face and aimed his weapon downrange again. She turned her attention back to Matt and Mueen, pulled out another extended mag, and continued to shoot at them. Shit. She was like the

Terminator. She turned around to check David, just as he was pretending to take aim at her. She didn't hesitate; she swiveled, and took aim at David.

Matt stood out from the side of the Suburban and positioned his rifle at eye level. He took a breath and winged her on the arm as she took a shot at David. Just enough to put her down and render her trigger hand unusable. As soon as she dropped, he brought up his gun to David. "Hold it right there."

David immediately tossed his empty gun to the sand and held his hands out to the side. "She shot me."

"Shut up," Matt said, ignoring him and approaching Maggie. "Hey Mags, how ya doin'?"

"Fuck you." She ground out, holding on to her arm. Well, he figured that was one for Harry, since it was obvious that one of Maggie's bullets had caused her wound. He looked back at Mueen, who was still holding the other guys at gunpoint. He frisked Maggie quickly and found a flick knife and a small Baretta at her ankle. He pocketed those and made his way to David, who was still standing. David opened his mouth.

"I am not talking to you, you fucking traitor," Matt said.

"Oh, come on, Boomer. I did all but take out a skywriter to tell you we were fucking with you." David's hand was stemming the weak flow of blood.

"What are you talking about?" Matt said, ripping his button-down off to wrap around his leg.

"I made sure your woolen socks to the west and your hangers were all messed up so you knew we'd searched your room. I all but left pointers to the bug... Told you I was keeping my *ear* to the *ground*. I had orders. I couldn't come out and tell you you were under surveillance. My people don't take too kindly to those who disobey direct orders. Not kindly at all."

"You killed a man. An old professor who was nothing to do with this. I know you did; you called him an old man before you'd even heard of him." Matt deliberately yanked the make-shift bandage around his legs, making David groan in pain.

"I didn't. Those fucking Eastern Europeans did." He looked back at the men Mueen was tying up. "They take photos of their kills. Yeah"—he groaned and leaned against Matt for a second—"they have a portfolio of people they killed to...I guess to prove they did the job. Like some kind of show-and-tell."

Relief washed over Matt. Everything he said made sense. Then he caught a whiff of... "Dude, are you drunk right now?"

"I hope so. God, I hope so." He hung his head and shut up.

Matt put an arm under his and led him back to David's Suburban. He shoved him in the backseat, but as he was about to slam the door on him, he said, "Watch out...she's on the move. And she has the keys to the truck."

Matt turned. Maggie was already almost to the trailer. Harry. Molly. *Fuck.*

Shit. Matt looked at his watch. They were nearly out of time.

* * *

While Matt and Mueen had distracted the patrols, Molly and Harry crept into the trailer. It wasn't empty.

"Jason?" Molly exclaimed. "What the hell?"

He was sitting on the cooler, hunched over Harry's laptop. He was also crying. "I can't...I can't get in. I don't know your password."

"Why are you trying to get into my laptop?" Harry said.

"Katherine told me I had to. She said she'd come back and kill me if I didn't. She's out there. Except. How did you get in without her seeing you? I'm going to die, aren't I?" His face creased up as if he was about to wail like a baby.

Molly and Harry exchanged looks. "It's okay, Jason. I'm here now," Harry said, trying to calm him down.

He didn't seem to hear her. He jumped off the cooler and made a beeline for the small window. "Oh my God. She's coming." He looked at the women with a desperate expression on his face. Then he turned back to the window. "She's coming." His voice quavered. "You've got to get me out of here.

"What's so scary about an archaeologist?" Harry asked. "I do remember right that she was in Professor Rapson's team, don't I?" Even as she said the words, she remembered that neither Molly nor she had ever seen a woman on his team.

"She told me I'd get rich. She said that her company would pay me fifty thousand dollars for your map. I thought it was harmless." His eyes were glued to the window. "I thought she liked me."

Harry stood behind him trying to see who it was. A woman in black headed toward them, clasping her arm. She turned to Molly.

"I'm guessing she came from one of the patrol cars."

"She has a gun. More than one. She…" Jason's chin quivered. "She put it in my mouth and pulled the trigger. Said she'd keep going until she found the one bullet with my name on it unless I'd help her."

Harry looked around the trailer. "We need to find a weapon. I don't know if she knows we are here."

Molly started looking through the empty cupboards that they never thought to stock with anything. Nothing. She turned and shrugged wordlessly.

"Okay, this will have to do." Harry banged on the bottom of

the cupboard shelves until they popped up. "We will shelve her if we have to," Harry said, trying to inject a little levity into the near-death situation. No one laughed. She didn't blame them.

"Don't leave me alone with her. Please," Jason begged.

Molly rolled her eyes at him and Harry could tell she was wondering what she'd ever seen in the man. "Don't worry, Jason. I brought you here, I'm going to be sure to take you back with me."

The first shot came through the side of the trailer and passed directly between Harry and Molly. They both jumped and looked at the hole it left in the rear of the trailer behind them. Then they dived for the floor. Molly grabbed Jason and pulled him down. So much for the shelving they were going to give her.

The door burst open and she stood there with a tiny gun that obviously packed a big punch. She stepped inside, and all three of the real archaeologists scrambled to each other and sat on the floor watching her. She pressed her gun to Harry's head. She didn't say anything, just stared at the open doorway and waited.

Harry didn't dare move. Her whole body went cold from the outside in, and she wondered whether she'd ever see her home again.

Chapter 25

Matt's heart stopped when he saw the gun to Harry's head. His thoughts immediately turned to the images of the hostage videos sometimes seen on news bulletins. Never before had it been someone he loved wincing away from the weapon.

Loved. *Hell yeah.*

"I'm sorry, Matt, but I have my orders," Maggie said in an emotionless voice. "I have to get the information from the laptop and deliver it to my bosses, who are arriving in"—she checked her watch—"ten hours."

Matt checked his own watch. Twenty minutes until they had to be ready. Maggie was also a loose end.

"Harry, just give Maggie the laptop," Matt said in the calmest voice he could muster. He hoped that by getting Harry to get the laptop, Maggie would at least take the gun from her head. But belying his voice was a fury that burned in his heart. *How dare she endanger Harry's life?*

"I th-thought her name was Katherine?" Jason said.

Harry ignored him and gave Maggie the computer.

"I'm not stupid. What's the password? He didn't know." She nodded toward the cowering Jason.

Harry hesitated, and then said, "Danny forever—four as in the number, all one word." Her eyes sought Matt's, but he looked away. Fuck. He couldn't believe he'd been this stupid. She was in love with Danny still, and nothing was going to drag her from the past. Even with a gun at her head. Enough. *Enough.* He was drawing a line under this whole trip. He was leaving her in *his* past.

"Thank you. Now, I'm sorry, but I have orders to kill you all." She raised her gun, and Matt lunged for her. As he made contact with her, a shot rang out, and a warm spray hit his face. Was it him? Had he been shot? He'd never been shot before but was pretty sure it would involve more pain.

He fell to the floor on top of Maggie, and took a second to assess. Had she killed someone in the trailer? He scrambled onto his knees. "Harry?"

"We're all fine." Her voice came softly as the echo of the gun died away.

He looked around. Maggie'd been shot in the head. He looked in the doorway. David was standing on one leg, aiming into the trailer with the gun Matt had dropped outside when he'd seen Harry in danger. He nodded at him. David nodded back.

"Mom, Dad? Can I keep him?" Molly had caught sight of David through the window. Matt thought she was probably in shock. Hoped. Hoped she was in shock.

* * *

Ten minutes later, Harry stood still, hands over her mouth in horror. She couldn't bring herself to look at the extent of the devastation. But then she peeked. Next to the huge burning crater were two men, sprawled out pools of blood beneath them. They looked as if they had been blown up and out by an explosion.

Embers glowed in the dark crater, and a few hundred-dollar bills were shredded and burning around the hole.

Matt was to her right, flat on his back, blood seeping from his eyes, nose, and mouth. It was a horror movie. Molly was at her feet, kneeling and bowing over as if she couldn't bear the smell of charred flesh.

In the moments that followed, she allowed herself to think of returning to her life without Matt. Spending her days and nights alone, or with some guy she'd picked up for fun. Trying to restore her name in her professional field. Was that all she wanted from life? Or would she risk something different?

"Hold it a minute more." Matt's voice came from the side of his mouth where the blood hadn't congealed.

"My knees hurt," complained Molly.

David sniggered, and then coughed as he inhaled sand.

"Everyone shut up!" Harry said through her hands. One thing was for sure. She was going to change all her passwords.

"You know, if I have to lie here in the sun for another minute pretending to be dead, I will, actually, be dead," David said.

"I won't let you die," Molly cooed, head still bowed.

Harry shook her head. This was the craziest thing she'd ever done. And she wasn't sure if she'd ever be able to tell anyone about it.

"And…we're done," Matt said, sitting up.

David pulled himself wincing into a semi-upright position and Molly shuffled over to him. "I can't believe this will work. How did it even occur to you?" he asked Matt.

"They did this in Europe in World War II to confuse the German surveillance aircraft. Their camouflage was a little more elaborate, though. They had stage backdrops painted as bomb craters and placed them over buildings that the Luftwaffe had targeted. When the surveillance planes flew over to assess the damage they'd inflicted, they took photos of what looked like a direct hit, and the bombers went on to different targets. Let's just hope it works the same way with high-resolution, low-orbiting satellite imagery."

"We still have to liberate the money before MGL sends more people," Harry said, hoping that Matt would at least look at her. But he instead looked back toward where they were going to dig. They'd set up the decoy a hundred feet or so away, just in case they couldn't extract the money in time.

Matt avoided Harry's eyes and turned to David. "You up for this?"

David held up his hand to show how steady it was. It was shaking. "Hell yeah. We are the Master Blasters," he said with a grin.

Matt held his hand out to David and helped him up. Mueen had already gotten five workers started on the digging. They hit the container pretty quickly. Molly and Harry had cut the sheets that had the bomb crater crudely painted on them and placed them around the container. On one side, the pallet had been damaged by the blast that Mueen had told them had brought down the aircraft. "You guys need to get away. Start putting the gear we brought into the Suburban, but keep it over there by the trailer," Matt told them all. God, she wished he'd just look at her.

"Be careful," Harry said.

He stared at her with an inscrutable expression. "We will." He stuck his fist out to David, still with his eyes on Harry. David knocked his fist on Matt's, and they both lay down on their stomachs facing the bomb.

As she walked away, Harry could hear them laughing together and trash-talking each other as they got to work on the device.

* * *

Twenty minutes and seven years' worth of trash talk later, the bomb was defused and the money was being loaded into the truck. David was sitting in the sand, rerigging the explosives with his watch as timer so that they could really blow up the hole they pretended they had earlier.

"I'm going to go make a call when we get back and get that sorted out," Matt said without elaborating.

"Can we talk?" Harry asked quietly. She needed to make this right.

"Yup."

"About the password. Both of them, actually. They've been that way for years…"

"You don't have to explain. You've been nothing but clear. Danny was… *is* the love of your life. It's okay. He's important to me, too. But there is no way I'm playing second fiddle to a dead man. Not that you ever asked me to. But I think it's best we just keep it professional from now on. All the"—he waved his hands around as if he didn't know what to say—"all the other stuff… well, we'll just pretend that didn't happen."

"But that's not what I want," she whispered, painfully aware that people were moving things around them.

"Harry. It's what *I* want. What I *need*." He stared at her for a second, and then picked up some shovels and slung them in the back of the truck on top of the money. "Mueen, we'll need these shovels tonight."

Mueen looked between them both and nodded, frowning.

His attitude had changed on a dime. His eyes no longer held the warmth they did when he'd looked at her before. He no longer jumped to get her things, to make her comfortable. Although she'd never asked him to do those things, she felt their absence. It was like the chill of fall after a hot summer.

She would make this right. She would explain how she felt later. When they were really alone. When this was all behind them.

Chapter 26

Matt made absolutely sure they weren't alone. As soon as they went back to the sheik's compound, he and Mueen made themselves at home in the sheik's office and made some phone calls.

Mueen alerted the police to the fact that there were two suspected assassins tied up at the dead professor's site, and got someone to pick up Matt, Molly, and Harry's belongings from the hotel. Matt also asked him to arrange flights for the next day for Molly. Jason had escaped back to the Majestic hotel and seemed too embarrassed to face any of them again. He needed Harry for the most important part of their mission.

Matt made one call to Jenks, and felt confident that everything he needed would be taken care of. His commander had seen the satellite feed and swore up and down that he'd been terrified that they were all dead. Jenks would file a report saying that they tripped the explosives and destroyed the container. Matt couldn't believe his ruse had worked. Now there was just one thing left to take care of.

* * *

Two hours later, Molly, Harry, Ain, David, and Mueen were at the couple's house, in the yard. David, Mueen, and Matt were saluting as four members of Ain's family, under Harry's careful supervision, lifted the crude wooden casket from the flower bed at the bottom of the garden.

They placed it on a little wheeled desk and rolled it out to a large truck. Harry asked them all to step back as she eased the lid partially off the coffin. Her whole body became heavy as she took in the contents. Lieutenant Grant Mather lay at peace. His uniform intact, his name tag still attached to his shirt, and dried flowers lying on his body. She turned slowly and nodded at Matt, her own grief reflected in his eyes. She replaced the lid and stepped back so that straps could be put around to secure everything in place for transport. It was carefully lifted into a large cargo box and put in the rear of the truck.

The truck took off, and the rest followed in David's Suburban. Harry became more and more aware that she was losing, if not already lost, Matt. He'd made it clear that he didn't want to see her, and she understood that it wasn't him being vindictive, just that she had made it impossible for him to believe that she could, maybe be, in love with him. Their bags had been packed by one of the sheik's men, and they were heading to the airport for good. All she had now was one day... one day in transit back to the States to persuade him. Persuade him of what, exactly, she still hadn't put into words in her own head.

Matt's head was quite rightly on his duties repatriating Mueen's copilot. She didn't think that he'd implicitly said so, but everyone's feeling was that he wasn't going to mention Mueen in his report. A report he'd admitted would go no further than his own commander.

She wasn't giving up on Matt entirely, though. When he'd been out of the truck, she swiped the address label tied on his backpack. It didn't have his home address, just his unit name and location. It was her Hail Mary if she couldn't get him to talk to her on the way home.

Harry was accompanying the Colonel's remains back to Dover, Delaware, as the acting anthropologist, and Matt was there as the recovery team leader. Commander Jenks had alerted the notification team, and she understood that his parents would be meeting them at Dover Air Force Base.

When they arrived at Baghdad Airport, Harry and Molly followed Matt and David through the doors of the terminal. The usual throng of people were there to meet each aircraft: families, friends, taxi drivers, and others looking for an opportunity to be of service to a weary traveler. Matt stopped abruptly and after a second, pulled her around front so she could see. The crowd in the terminal was parting like the Red Sea. Coming through were four men. Walking with the same confidence as Matt. Chins up, eyeing the crowd. Her breath caught.

None of them was in uniform, but they all carried the same military rucks; sand-colored backpacks that bulged in different directions. The leader of the group was in cargo pants and a Hawaiian shirt.

The last time she had seen them together was at Danny's funeral. She flashed back to them in their dress blues, presenting her with the flag that had been draped over Danny's coffin. Matt's old unit. The four remaining men from the EOD squad. They'd come to help.

Her heart filled. Like her whole body was filled with love for

these men, who put honor and family above everything. Both
hands flew to her mouth, as if covering it would force back in
all the emotion that was too big for her body. Overflowing from
every pore, and every tear duct. They'd told her that they would
come if she ever needed anything. She'd never thought to call
them for anything. But they'd come anyway.

When their eyes lit upon Matt and her, their faces broke into
smiles. Backpacks were dropped, man hugs and backslaps were
exchanged. The tallest of them took the measure of her in a second. It was Liam…something. He'd been the one to actually hand
her the flag. He'd cried as he'd done it. He stood for a second in
front of her, making her embarrassed for the tears and snot.

"Hell, Marko, I know we look bad, there's no need to cry.
Don't get too close to Justin, either. He smells like hell, and that
will make you cry."

Harry laughed, hiccuped, and held out her hand to Liam.

"Screw that," he said as he wrapped his arms around her waist
and hugged her, lifting her from the floor. "It's good to see you
again," he said, putting her back on terra firma. He stepped back
and reintroduced Mark, Bill, and Justin, who had a red stain
down the front of his shirt.

"Bloody Mary and turbulence," he explained ruefully.

"Thank you so much for coming to help us get the…cargo…
to the right places. I don't know what to say," she said.

Liam frowned. "You don't have to say anything. Ever." He
bent to pick up his rucksack and launched it across his shoulders.

"You," Liam said, pointing at David. "You went to the dark
side. You are Darth Vader to me." He eyed him with a squint.

"Yeah, I know," David said, eyes cast down.

"And you got shot by a chick. Anyone else here been shot by a
chick?" He looked around.

Everyone shook their heads.

Matt let David off the hook by saying, "This is Mueen, and he will be your tour director while you're here. Do good. I've got to take a friend home."

All four of their faces fell into solemnity. "Fly safe, man," Liam said, sticking his hand out. Matt shook all their hands and watched them go with Mueen. David grabbed Molly and said a few fierce words to her before limping out with the guys.

After hugs, Molly headed off to the charter airline that would fly her and all their equipment back to the U.S. via Paris.

Matt led Harry to a desk at the other side of the terminal, where after showing their IDs at the counter, they were allowed through to the tarmac. Army personnel were carefully putting the casket into the belly of the large military aircraft.

Harry shielded her eyes from the dying sun and took a moment to watch their precise movements. They marched slowly from the truck to the aircraft, holding the box on their shoulders. She wondered if this was how they'd brought Danny home to her. The question didn't stab her with pain, like the thought of him used to. He was a part of her. His loss didn't hurt like before, but he was always there. How had she not noticed that it didn't ache anymore? When had she stopped waking up thinking of Danny? When had she started considering a future that didn't involve living alone?

Matt stood at attention next to her, watching Lieutenant Colonel Mather's progress. It was their job to get him home and hand him over to his family. Tears seeped out of her eyes as she imagined how his parents would feel, having him home at last. She glanced sideways at Matt. This was a good job he had. Honorable.

As the casket disappeared from view, the distinctive ring of the sat phone Matt had commandeered sounded. Harry put her bag down and waited for him to take the call. A few other passengers got on the plane using the rear ramp. There was going to be no beverage or food service on this flight—just whatever food Ain had put into a cooler for them. There were no passenger seats, just benches along the sides of the fuselage with seat belts attached.

As Matt paced, taking his call, she tried to figure out the time she had to...urgh, she didn't know exactly what she was going to do. Convince Matt that she wasn't still holding a torch for Danny? And then she heard the tail end of his conversation and went cold.

"EOD? Yes, commander. I'd be all over that. I was just thinking that I wanted to go back...Yes, sir. Absolutely. I understand."

Harry's breath caught in her throat. EOD? He was going back to EOD? How could he? Streams of ice ran through her veins. She couldn't make sense of what was happening to her. Was she being punished for considering a future with someone else?

When he hung up and picked up both their bags, she laid a hand on his arm. "Are you leaving JPAC?"

His expression closed. "That's need to know. And you don't need to know."

Chapter 27

A few hours into the flight, his jaw was aching. Matt took a breath and tried to relax, tried to ease the tension that pulsed through him in time with the throb of the engine. Every nerve was twanging with the noise of being on a plane. He concentrated on every breath, every beat of his heart to exercise control over his anxiety from the constant background noise. Harry was sitting opposite him, facing him from the other side of the aircraft. She'd been staring at him since they'd climbed on board. That wasn't helping matters.

Goddammit. He didn't understand women at all. He rolled his neck to alleviate some pain there, too. The aircraft had about ten other people in its passenger area—a couple of soldiers in uniform and the rest in civilian clothes. Probably from the embassy or some other government office.

He met Harry's eyes and could see the wheels turning inside. He should have just come out and told her that he was heading back to EOD school to help train the new technicians. That made him a horrible person, and he was fine with that. His insides were beaten up, and his brain was punishing him for allowing himself to get attached to making love to Danny's wife. The past three years he'd had maybe two serious mental shitstorms that he could directly attribute to watching his friend die. This week he'd had three. And she was the reason.

He was punishing her for something that wasn't her fault. He knew that. But he needed to keep her at arm's length if he was going to keep his hands off her. Because God knew, as soon as his hands were on her, in her hair, feeling her…well, sanity flew out of the window. And keeping his sanity close was the only way he knew to walk away from her.

He needed his head to get back to the place it was a week ago. *But where was that?* In some void between finding missing bodies and picking up women. He scrubbed his hands over his face. Fuck. Fuck it all to hell.

Something jogged him and he looked up. Harry had ninja'd her way over the expanse of the plane and was strapping herself into the space next to him. Crap.

"Are you all right?" he asked.

"Are you? Or are you crazy?" she demanded, eyes flashing.

He groaned. "What are you talking about?" He knew. He knew what was coming. He braced for impact.

"Are you even kidding me about going back to EOD? Is that your idea of a joke, or…or is it some kind of way to get back at me?"

"Even my career decisions are about you now? You take the cake, lady."

Her face flushed at that. "How many times had you thought about going back to EOD before this week?" she asked.

Her voice had risen, and he looked around at the other inhabitants of the aircraft. At least two were looking on at their exchange with some amusement. He flicked the fastener of the seat belt and stabbed a finger toward the front of the plane where the only rest room was. He knew it would be quieter in front of the engines and there would be less need to shout in front of everyone.

As soon as they got to the relative quiet of the place where a galley would be in a commercial plane, he tried to head her off. "I don't want to discuss my career options with you. I don't want to discuss anything with you."

"Is this still about the passwords? I'm sorry about that. They've been my passwords for years. I never thought to change them, never imagined my choice would affect anyone." She said the words softly, barely audible over the noise. His nerves jangled as the ambient noise made him strain to hear her.

"That was just the icing on the cake, Harry. It's everything. Everything. Relationships, sex. It should be easy. You and me? We have too many obstacles on too many levels. You're my best friend's wife. All my career choices have been driven by the experience of watching him die in front of me. All of them. My personal relationships have been driven by..." He stopped, unwilling to actually verbalize his "hit it and quit it" past.

Past?

The plane passed through some cloud, which made sunlight flash through one of the tiny windows. He winced against the flickering light, and in that split second he lost the tight grip on his brain. The aircraft started shaking, and he tried to get Harry to safety. He grabbed her arm.

"It's okay, Matt. I've got you." He felt her fingers cool against his neck, and then forehead. "We're fine. Everything's fine."

He opened his eyes and found hers. She looked concerned. But he felt fine. "What happened?"

Her hands left his skin and slipped down his shoulders to his arms. "You started shaking, like you had a fever. Does that happen a lot?"

He shook his head. "No...I don't know."

"I'm so sorry. I'm so sorry. I feel like I've caused all this tension and stress for you. But this will stop now. I'm sorry. I just wanted to tell you that I didn't mean to hurt you, or take you to a place that you didn't want to go."

She slipped her hand into his. And it felt so good. So, so good. His heart rate steadied under the mere touch of her hand.

"You never once took me somewhere I didn't want to go," Matt said simply. He squeezed her hand and released it. He needed distance from her to get himself back together. "I just can't do this right now. You understand?"

Her chin wobbled under his gaze. He raised his hand to touch it, to smooth out the hurt on her face, and stroked the side of her face. Her soft skin felt like velvet under his fingers. Unable to stop himself, he cupped her warm cheek and closed his eyes as she turned her lips to his palm and kissed him. He couldn't walk away. He wanted to walk back to his seat, fasten his seat belt, and concentrate on keeping his head together. But no part of his body wanted any part of that. He brought her face around toward his and leaned down.

His lips traced her forehead, his hand smoothed her hair. He kissed her cheeks and eyes, feeling a dampness that wasn't there before. When he reached her lips, it wasn't passion driving his kiss. It wasn't his dick leading the charge. It was his heart.

His heart, dammit.

He framed her face between his hands and pulled away. He held her gaze for a moment, trying to remember this feeling, how she looked. Trying to etch her in his brain.

He dropped his hands, took a deep breath, and walked away.

Went straight back to his seat, closed his eyes, and tried to breathe through the empty feeling in his stomach.

* * *

Harry chose a seat at the front of the aircraft so she wouldn't have to look at Matt for the rest of the flight. A quick glance at him before she sat confirmed his complete ambivalence to her; his eyes were closed and he seemed to be completely relaxed.

She wished he would open up to her, but clearly there was more going on inside than he'd ever let on. Maybe it was better to walk away unscathed. To chalk it up as a learning experience. To be more open to love. Maybe slightly open to love.

It was too much. She closed her eyes and allowed herself to relax into the slight movement the aircraft made as it flew them home. Flew Colonel Mather home. He'd been away too long.

Harry awoke to the grinding sound of the aircraft wheels being lowered. She swallowed hard to release the pressure in her ears. She stretched to ease the tightness in her muscles and automatically looked around for Matt. He was talking to a crew member, pointing at the other passengers. She figured he was probably going over the protocol for the removal of the casket.

She watched him as he spoke, taking advantage of the fact that his attention wasn't on her. He looked so strong, so sure of himself, but she'd seen a chink in his armor. Maybe she'd even caused it.

The plane landed and the un-uniformed passengers were disembarked into a van on the flight line. The ramp came back up, and the plane taxied to the tarmac in front of the main building. Harry stood and tried to hang as far back as she could, not wanting to intrude on this dignified transfer of the colonel back to his parents.

The aircraft ramp was lowered again, and an honor guard of airmen came into the aircraft to prepare the casket. Emotion flooded through her as they wrapped it in an American flag. This is how she met Danny on his return to the U.S. She shrank farther away from them and covered her mouth with her hands. *Don't cry. Don't cry.*

The honor guard lifted the container and slow-marched it down the ramp, as three airmen saluted. Watching the solemnity choked her. But it wasn't about Danny. Not anymore. It was the respect and honor these young airmen paid to someone they had never met or known. It moved her. She wondered how many of these operations Matt had witnessed.

The casket was carefully put into what looked like a military ambulance and was driven slowly to the building. Only then did Matt look back at her. "Are you all right?" he asked.

She nodded. "It was a moving ceremony." She picked up her bag and went toward him.

"We can walk to the back of the building from here and Mather's parents will be given the opportunity to talk to us, as the people who found him, if they want to. Is that okay with you?"

"Of course. That's why I came. I think I may have a...fairly unique perspective."

She absolutely swore that he extended his arm as if he was offering his hand to take, but he clenched his fist and dropped his arm back to his side. "Let's go," he said.

They sat silently in a bare waiting room for about twenty minutes before someone came to get them. They were led into the chapel complex, then another waiting room, this one furnished with armchairs and paintings. A couple dressed in their Sunday best held hands while they looked at the flag-draped coffin.

"Mr. and Mrs. Mather. May I introduce Senior Master Sergeant Matt Stanning, from our JPAC unit, and Dr. Henrietta Markowitz. They supervised the recovery of your son."

They shook hands. "I'm so sorry for your loss," Harry said.

Mrs. Mather smiled. "Thank you for bringing him home, Dr. Markowitz. And for taking the time to speak with us."

"Please call me Harry," she said. "I'm so glad we were able to."

Mr. Mather spoke in a thick-with-emotion voice. "What can you tell us about how he died?"

Harry looked at Matt.

"I'm afraid we—"

"I know. I know. Grant wouldn't want you to break any classified rules or anything. I don't mean what he was doing when he died, just how he died."

Matt seemed to be at a loss of what to say.

"Someone very kind was looking after him when he died. He was being cared for. I promise. He didn't die alone."

Mrs. Mather's chin quivered just the smallest bit as she nodded. "Thank you. Thank you for telling us that. It means a lot. Really. More than you know."

"I do know. I was in your exact position seven years ago when someone brought my husband home to this very air force base."

"Oh, my dear. You are much too young to have gone through that. I'm so sorry. At least we've had time to grieve. We had to accept years ago that Grant wouldn't be coming home." She reached out and put her hand on Harry's shoulder. "There were so many things he wanted to do, so many dreams. Tragedies like this remind us how short life can be, how precious." She sniffed and blinked rapidly, casting her gaze at the ceiling for a few seconds as if collecting herself.

Harry blinked back tears of her own. "You're absolutely right," she replied. "I think…I think I'd forgotten that." The more Mrs.

Mather's words sunk in, the more Harry realized that she'd been totally passive since Danny died. She'd let things happen to her, never really *making* things happen.

A protocol officer came in to lead the couple away. They said their good-byes, and left Matt and Harry alone in the waiting room.

She put her hands on her hips. "So what now?"

Chapter 28

She looked at him expectantly, her hands on hips, her head cocked. Like she was daring him. Daring him to feel, to accept a mission that would only end in heartbreak for both of them.

"I can't be the man you need," he said. "You deserve so much more, so much life."

"Well, as much as I appreciate being told what I need, you're wrong. I do need you." She frowned. "No. I don't need you. I want you. And I want to need you. Shit, this is confusing. *You* are making it confusing, Matt, and it shouldn't be. I'm just a woman who wants to be with you. I don't care if it ends tomorrow, or next month, or maybe next year if we decide it's too difficult, but I'm damned if I'm going to walk away without even trying. That's...*lame.*"

He inched toward the tiny dynamo standing in front of him, all piss and vinegar. "You're calling me lame?" he said, almost standing over her.

"If you walk away for no good reason," she countered, standing her ground.

"I have reasons—"

"I said *good* reasons. You heard what the woman said. Life is too short. Yes, I'm nervous about you putting yourself in danger with the EOD. But I don't want to regret not trying."

He slowly brushed his hand over her hair and wound one soft tendril around his fingertip. She was electricity to him. Powerful and necessary and dangerous. But he could handle dangerous. He dealt with it every day.

"I'm not going back to EOD. I'm going back to the school to teach. To train airmen to be better than we were. To do better." He grinned. "To blow more shit up."

"Really?" she whispered.

"Really."

She paused. "Well, then I've made my point."

"Oh, and what was that?"

"There is nothing between us that two functioning adults can't figure out, and I'm not going to put up with your shit anymore."

"Oh, really?" He leaned forward and kissed her neck.

She sighed and wove her fingers through his hair, pressing her whole body against him. Yeah, he was a goner. He wasn't going to leave here without her, or at least without a plan to get her.

He picked her up, threw her over his shoulder, and strode out of the room.

"Where are you taking me?"

"Out of the chapel. I don't want to compound my sins." He took her to a flight planning office which was thankfully deserted at this hour.

She scrambled down from his shoulder and smiled up at him. Killer smile. He grabbed her waist and lifted her onto the counter. Standing between her legs, he took her face in his hands. "This isn't going to be easy. I can tell you that now. I need to fix my head, fix my life."

She looked deep into his eyes. "We're both a little broken. But I don't want to hide anymore. I want you in my life. However hard it is."

"Guess what?" he said as he bent to claim her mouth. "It's pretty damned hard right now."

The sound of her laughter as he touched his lips to hers intoxicated him as much as her kiss.

Epilogue

Two months later

Harry scrabbled in her armrest to plug the headphones in. A serious news anchor was speaking when she finally got it into the jack. They'd been covering the MGL Security story for weeks now, and the government had just concluded its investigation into the events in Iraq.

"And in a 'you-couldn't-make-it-up twist,' the famous philanthropic organization, the Megellin Foundation, is actually owned, through multiple shell corporations, by MGL Security, a private military company contracted by the government to provide security in Iraq. In a statement given today by the attorney general, it's become clear that the charitable foundation has been using renowned archaeologists to survey ancient sites and then making off with any artifacts and treasure they find. It really seems like an Indiana Jones movie, doesn't it? We're going over to Cindy Carter in Washington D.C., who is speaking with Molly Solent, an archaeologist instrumental in the downfall of MGL Security..."

Harry smiled and clasped a hand over her chest to see Molly looking so authoritative and lovely on-screen. She was going to miss seeing her every day.

Matt had come back to Boston with her for two days before flying off to Florida to take his place at the EOD school. They talked on the phone when they could, but she'd been busy with the paperwork to help wrap up the Megellin investigation, and Matt didn't exactly have a lot of free time, either. Or maybe the distance was already affecting them. Every night, she fell asleep dreaming of him, longing for his arms around her again. But what if he didn't feel the same way? A tiny shaft of worry threaded through her as she took in the enormity of what she was doing: risking her heart for someone she only hoped wanted her full-time.

They had talked about her moving down there, but he hadn't explicitly invited her. And new Harry wasn't waiting for an invitation. There were too many what-ifs in life. She didn't want this to be one of hers.

She'd either finally heal her heart... or go down in flames.

* * *

The wave broke perfectly, and he sprung up on his board. The sounds of the ocean became white noise as he coasted through the curl. It wasn't a big wave, just enough to bring him some peace of mind. He'd resumed surfing after his therapist suggested he try meditation. Uh, no. In a compromise, they'd agreed on surfing.

It had worked. Every time he took his board into the sea, he felt cleansed, pure of mind, even. Like it strengthened his ability to cope with everything that had happened in his life.

As he jumped off his board ready to paddle back out to catch the next wave, he saw her on the beach. Blond hair blowing in the breeze, eyes steady on him. Well, maybe not entirely cleansed of her. His imagination was still playing tricks on him.

He shook his head and paddled back out. While he waited for the next one, he couldn't help but look back at the beach to see if he could still see her. No. Of course not. His therapist had told him that everything that had happened to him, Danny's death, his constant flashbacks would ease but may manifest in vivid dreams. And he'd already had plenty of them. Waking so hard, and longing for her, that his morning routine had involved ice-cold showers. So he wasn't entirely surprised that he'd thought he saw her.

And then he did see her. He'd thought she'd disappeared, but she'd only sat down on the sand. What the…?

He sat up on his board and shielded his eyes from the sun. Was it really, truly her? Holy crap. The next wave was cresting. He jumped up and rode it to shore, his eyes never leaving her, in case…well, in case she was a mirage, a hallucination. As he got closer, picking up his board and walking from the sea, he was absolutely 100 percent sure it was her. She smiled at him, and his heart about broke through his chest wall.

"You're a long way from home," he said in what he hoped was a nonchalant voice.

She removed her sunglasses and held wisps of hair back from her face. "I…er, I had a hankering for the ocean," she said.

Matt picked up his towel and wiped his face. "You live in Boston. I hear the Cape is nice this time of year." Yeah, she had to say it. He wasn't going to allow her to hedge around this one. If she was all-in, she had to say so, even though every cell in his body wanted him to reach out, pick her up, and never let her go.

"Yeah, it is," she said, looking up the beach. "But you're not at the Cape."

He couldn't help a grin breaking out. "No. I'm not."

She swallowed hard, and he began to feel guilty at making her sweat. But then she made it…everything…worthwhile. "And I want to be where you are." Her eyes held his for a second and then dropped away. "I know we were taking things slow, but I'm kind of done with that now. I didn't want to wait to start 'us' anymore. I want to start it now. Every time I think about my future, in Greece, at home, on vacation…you're there with me. I can't seem to visualize my future without you."

He placed two fingers under her chin and tipped her face back up to his. "Then I want you to be where I am, too."

Her smile would have lit the entire beach had it not been bathed in early-morning sunlight already.

"How long are you staying?" he asked, his eyes lingering at her lips.

"I only brought a carry-on with bikinis, shorts, and t-shirts," she said, biting her lip.

He placed a gentle, yet utterly claiming kiss on her forehead. "You could stay for months, years even, with just those things."

She wrapped her arms around him. "I know."

Please turn the page for an excerpt of the previous book in
Emmy Curtis's sexy military romance Alpha Ops series

Over the Line

Available now!

Chapter 1

"Alone at last," Walker whispered as he crouched next to Beth. Dust flew up as the crack of a bullet hitting the ground ricocheted around the valley. He flattened himself next to her.

"You are *shit* at taking orders," she hissed back.

He ignored her as he tried to figure out where the shots were coming from. If he could just neutralize the immediate threat, he could patch her up and get her to safety. His blood had flashed ice-cold when she radioed that she'd been hit. And she'd still been laying down covering fire for the guys when he'd found her. If she was the first taste of females in combat, bring it on.

A pool of dark blood glistened in the hazy moonlight, expanding and trickling across the sand as he watched.

Crap.

Their simple mission of relieving another patrol group had gone to hell in a handbasket. Another shot echoed around them, and this time Walker was ready to identify the telltale muzzle flash. As soon as he saw it, he swung his gun and sent a shot downrange toward the insurgent.

Silence. He took that as a good sign.

"Okay, Sergeant. Turn over so I can look at that leg."

Beth grunted but complied, biting back a moan as she did.

Walker's heart dropped when he saw that her BDU pants were completely soaked with blood. A lot of it. *Shit*. Maybe the bullet had nicked an artery. He grabbed his knife and cut away the pant leg to expose the wound. It was about two inches below her panty line. And blood was still pumping out in rhythm with her heartbeat.

He undid her belt and pulled it off. No way was he going to let her die in this crappy valley, in the middle of Shithole City, Bumfuck. No fucking way.

As he slid the belt around the top of her thigh, trying not to touch anything that could get him court-martialed, one of the Strike Eagles he had called for screamed overhead. He threw himself over Beth, and waited for the bombs to drop.

They exploded with precision, of course. Walker had been the one to give them the coordinates. That was his job. The only air force guy on the team, he was the one who communicated with the aircraft patrolling the skies above the war zone. The only one who could give the bombers precise targets. The valley lit up with orange fire as they detonated. Rocks and scree sprinkled them, sounding like heavy rain, feeling like stones.

That should keep the Taliban out of his hair for a bit. He made to get up and realized how close to Beth's face his was. He hesitated for a split second. A bad, bad second. He'd been deployed with her unit for a couple of months and had spent most of the time dreaming about her at night, and trying to ignore those dreams by day.

He swallowed, and went back to business. "I have to tourniquet your leg. It's going to hurt like a fucker," he said as he fas-
tened the belt as high on her thigh as he could manage. "Just
think, all this time I wanted to see your panties, and finally…"

Beth opened her mouth, probably to give him hell, and he
used the distraction to pull the belt tight.

"You bastard," she ground out between gritted teeth.

The wound stopped pumping blood and he silently thanked
whoever was looking out for them upstairs. He grabbed the first-
aid kit from his pack and took out gauze and dark green ban-
dages. A shot sounded again, and sand flew up just inches away
from his foot.

Shit.

Walker threw himself down again, this time lying between
her legs, face about five inches from her wound. Which meant it
was seven inches from her…

"Well, this is awkward," he murmured. It worked, and in relief
he heard her gasp a laugh.

"Next time…buy me dinner…first, all right?" she said
between pants of Lamaze-type breathing.

He laughed quietly. "I've got to get you out of here first. Then
I promise I will." He loosened the tourniquet, and watched to
see if the blood flow had stopped. It hadn't, but it wasn't pumping out as it had been before. He tightened it and vowed not to
check again.

"Walker," she ground out. "I have a letter. It's in my pants
pocket." She groaned as if she was trying to get control over the
pain. "Take it out before it gets soaked in blood. Make sure my
sister gets it if I…don't make it."

He didn't waste time placating her; he stuffed his hand into
her thigh pocket and grabbed the papers in there. He found

the letter and stuffed it in his own pocket, before replacing the notebook and loose papers back in hers. "Got it. I'll look after it. But I'm going to do everything I can to get you home to her, okay?"

"Look!" Beth grimaced as she propped herself up on one elbow and pointed up the valley where they had left their truck. A huge cloud of sand was making its way toward them, seemingly in slow motion. She made as if to get up, but fell back down with a moan as soon as she tried her leg.

The impending sandstorm made up his mind. They couldn't get stuck in it—Beth would die in all likelihood. If they didn't move now, the storm would be on them, and no rescue would be able to get to them until it dissipated. No time for second-guessing.

A cloud passed in front of the moon, and Walker instinctively jumped up. "Put your weight on your good leg." He held her opposite hand as if they were about to shake hands, and he pulled her up. "Come on, Garcia. Walk it off."

She breathed a laugh as he bent his knees and gently slid her over his shoulder in a fireman's carry, so her good leg bore the brunt of pressure against his shoulder. She wriggled pretty weakly in protest.

"What the fuck? Put me down. I can walk," she said, her words not reflected by the strain in her voice.

Yeah, not so much. "Sure you can, sweetheart…I mean Sergeant. But we need to run. Are you going to stay with me?"

"I've got your six," she whispered.

He launched his pack on his other shoulder and took off, away from the sandstorm. He knew he could outrun it—it was slow-moving—but the quicker he could get her to a reasonable landing zone, the quicker the helicopters would land and get her to a hospital.

The cloud passed the moon and in the sudden light they were sitting ducks. Another shot rang out, whizzing past so close he could feel it rip the air next to his face. Beth's stomach tensed muscles against his shoulder and she pulled herself up. One hell of a soldier. One hell of a woman.

She let off three shots as he ran, and then she flopped back down. "Got him," she said. And then there was silence except for his own breathing that filled his head. Blood pounded in his ears as he ran. Blood pumping, and breath puffing.

In out, in out, nearly there, nearly there.

His muscles strained under her weight, and the eighty pounds of their combined body armor, but he'd trained for this, and frankly, it wasn't his first rodeo. It was his eighth. His legs kept pumping toward safety.

He hoped.

The familiar *whop whop* of a helicopter penetrated his thoughts, as well as the more constant gunshots as he neared the last of their vehicles. Five soldiers were on the ground, firing their weapons into the hills opposite them.

He skidded to a halt and laid Beth down. He dropped alongside her and asked for a sit rep from the guys.

"Marks took one to the face. We lost him. There seem to be about eight TBs left in the hillside, but they're not giving up. Only small arms fired, so I figured the helo can land over there to the right of the valley entrance." The soldier pointed to the only real possible landing zone for the choppers.

"I have to go clear the LZ, Beth. I'll be back." He looked at her but she didn't look back. Eyes closed and barely breathing, she looked like she had already checked out. His heart clenched.

No. Fucking. Way. He pulled the tourniquet tight again, and started CPR. "Hey, you." He slapped the nearest soldier on his helmet. "I need you to do CPR while I clear the landing zone, okay? Keep the tourniquet tight."

The soldier took over without question. And then realized who it was. "Shit, is this Garcia? Oh man, my wife will kill me if I let her die," he said.

"So will I. Keep that thought in the very front of your mind. I'll be back in a few." He hesitated for a second. Could he trust the soldier with her? Everything in him wanted to stay and breathe life into her himself, but he was the only one who could talk the pararescuers in, and the only one who could clear a landing zone to the pilots' satisfaction.

Walker grabbed his radio and one of the soldiers' flashlights, and ran to the potential LZ. He walked the square, checking for IEDs or anything suspicious. He didn't think there would be, because the convoy had passed over this area on their way into the valley. He could still see their tire tracks. But it was better to be safe than sorry. As he paced, he couldn't stop thinking about Beth. How pale and lifeless she looked in the moonlight, how shallow her breathing, and how totally opposite that was to how she normally was: vibrant, prickly, beautiful, and strong.

The gentle *whop whop* of the helicopters became much louder as he finalized checking the LZ. He took out his radio.

"This is Playboy. PJs come in."

There were a few seconds of silence, during which he checked his radio for loose wires. Then, "This is PJ one, Playboy. How're we looking?"

"We have five able soldiers, one KIA, and one seriously injured. I've set up the landing zone at these coordinates." He rattled off a series of numbers.

"Can you light it up?"

"Roger that." Walker snapped some green chem lights from

his pocket, and threw them to the corners of the cleared landing zone. He would normally use flares, but he didn't want to give the Taliban an invitation to pick the PJs as their new target. Once it was clear the helo was good to land, he sprinted back to Beth. *Please, God. I'll do anything if you just let me get her to the hospital alive.*

The second trail helicopter opened fire into the hills, backing up the guys on the ground. Two Combat Rescue Officers ran from the helicopter toward them, weapons drawn. They took one look at Beth and started work on her. They secured her tourniquet and put an oxygen mask over her face.

Walker stood back and let them run with her back to the helo. His heart rate finally normalized, but the clenched fist in his stomach did not fade. Following the others to safety, all he could see was Beth's white face, and he wondered if she would live to have the promised dinner with him. As he unclenched his fists to climb into the Pave Hawk helo, he realized his fingers were crossed.

About the Author

Emmy Curtis is an editor and a romance writer. An ex-pat Brit, she quells her homesickness with Cadbury Flakes and Fray Bentos pies. She's lived in London, Paris, and New York and has settled, for the time being, in North Carolina. When not writing, Emmy loves to travel with her military husband and take long walks with their Lab. All things considered, her life is chock-full of hoot, just a little bit of nanny. And if you get that reference...well, she already considers you kin.

Learn more at:
EmmyCurtis.com
Twitter, @EmmyCurtis19
Facebook.com/EmmyCurtisAuthor